Micah had thought he knew this woman he'd been hired to protect—but she kept catching him by surprise.

Like that moment when they'd accidentally collided, and he'd felt a quick rush of heat at her touch. That touch had disturbed him more than he cared to admit.

He had his work cut out for him. He was going to have to stick to Prudence Street like glue until this was over.

And if it killed him, he was going to have to put that little collision out of his mind. The thought of the way she'd felt pressed against him still grabbed him by the heart. Not a good thing when he was being paid to see to her safety.

He'd have to remind himself, often, that he'd been hired as her *bodyguard*—not her lover....

Dear Reader,

The year is almost over, but the excitement continues here at Intimate Moments. Reader favorite Ruth Langan launches a new miniseries, THE LASSITER LAW, with *By Honor Bound.* Law enforcement is the Lassiter family legacy—and love is their future. Be there to see it all happen.

Our FIRSTBORN SONS continuity is almost at an end. This month's installment is *Born in Secret,* by Kylie Brant. Next month Alexandra Sellers finishes up this six-book series, which leads right into ROMANCING THE CROWN, our new twelve-book Intimate Moments continuity continuing the saga of the Montebellan royal family. THE PROTECTORS, by Beverly Barton, is one of our most popular ongoing miniseries, so don't miss this seasonal offering, *Jack's Christmas Mission.* Judith Duncan takes you back to the WIDE OPEN SPACES of Alberta, Canada, for *The Renegade and the Heiress,* a romantic wilderness adventure you won't soon forget. Finish up the month with *Once Forbidden...* by Carla Cassidy, the latest in her miniseries THE DELANEY HEIRS, and *That Kind of Girl,* the second novel by exciting new talent Kim McKade.

And in case you'd like a sneak preview of next month, our Christmas gifts to you include the above-mentioned conclusion to FIRSTBORN SONS, *Born Royal,* as well as *Brand-New Heartache,* award-winning Maggie Shayne's latest of THE OKLAHOMA ALL-GIRL BRANDS. See you then!

Yours,

Leslie J. Wainger
Executive Senior Editor

Please address questions and book requests to:
Silhouette Reader Service
U.S.: 3010 Walden Ave., P.O. Box 1325, Buffalo, NY 14269
Canadian: P.O. Box 609, Fort Erie, Ont. L2A 5X3

By Honor Bound

RUTH LANGAN

Silhouette®

INTIMATE MOMENTS™

Published by Silhouette Books

America's Publisher of Contemporary Romance

SILHOUETTE BOOKS

ISBN 0-373-27181-6

BY HONOR BOUND

Copyright © 2001 by Ruth Ryan Langan

All rights reserved. Except for use in any review, the reproduction
or utilization of this work in whole or in part in any form by any
electronic, mechanical or other means, now known or hereafter
invented, including xerography, photocopying and recording, or in
any information storage or retrieval system, is forbidden without
the written permission of the editorial office, Silhouette Books,
300 East 42nd Street, New York, NY 10017 U.S.A.

All characters in this book have no existence outside the imagination of
the author and have no relation whatsoever to anyone bearing the same
name or names. They are not even distantly inspired by any individual
known or unknown to the author, and all incidents are pure invention.

This edition published by arrangement with Harlequin Books S.A.

® and TM are trademarks of Harlequin Books S.A., used under license.
Trademarks indicated with ® are registered in the United States Patent
and Trademark Office, the Canadian Trade Marks Office and in other
countries.

Visit Silhouette at www.eHarlequin.com

Printed in U.S.A.

RUTH LANGAN

is an award-winning and bestselling author. Her books have been finalists for the Romance Writers of America's RITA Award. Over the years, she has given dozens of print, radio and TV interviews, including some for *Good Morning America* and *CNN News,* and has been quoted in such diverse publications as the *The Wall Street Journal, Cosmopolitan* and the *Detroit Free Press.* Married to her childhood sweetheart, she has raised five children and lives in Michigan, the state where she was born and raised.

Bryon, this one's for you.
And as always, for Tom, my own special bodyguard.

Prologue

The windows of the limousine were tinted so no one could see the occupants inside. Twelve-year-old Micah Lassiter sat on the seat facing his mother and grandfather. Sandwiched between them was his five-year-old brother, Cameron, who was staring out at the crowd with wide-eyed wonder. On either side of Micah were his ten-year-old brother, Donovan, and his eight-year-old sister, Mary Brendan.

Nobody spoke. And except for Cameron, nobody seemed to notice the long lines of uniformed men who stood at attention as the limousine came to a halt at the curb. The door was opened, and Kate Lassiter was helped out, followed by her father-in-law, Kieran, who turned to his oldest grandson.

"Micah, you see to your sister and brothers."

"Yes, sir." Taking charge was second nature for Micah. Firmly grasping his little brother's hand, he followed his elders up the steps of the cathedral, signaling for Bren and Donovan to follow.

As they climbed the steps, they passed through a tunnel of dark uniforms, men who had served with their father, whose faces were familiar to them, and yet on this day, oddly different. Today there were no sly winks, no wide smiles. Instead, the faces reflected pain, sadness, even anger.

At the entrance to the cathedral, they halted. The flag-draped casket was wheeled into position. And then, while the organ began the opening notes of a majestic hymn, they walked up the aisle, past relatives and friends, past strangers, some of them wearing shabby street garb, others honored dignitaries who had come to pay tribute to the man who had given his life for his friend and partner.

The service for Riordan Lassiter, son, husband, father and much-decorated police sergeant, was long and somber in tone. There were endless speeches about his courage and heroism. But his twelve-year-old son Micah couldn't keep his mind on the speakers. He found himself thinking about the man behind the badge. The handsome Irish face, with that shock of jet-black hair and eyes bluer than a summer sky. Eyes that could twinkle with humor or freeze the heart of an errant child. The silly jokes Riordan Lassiter had shared with his wife and children. Pizza at midnight, just for the fun of it. Root-beer floats in the summertime on the big front porch. He'd had a way of lightening the burden of a young boy with just a wink and a nudge of his elbow.

Did any of these strangers know Riordan Lassiter, the man? The man his wife, Kate, loved above all else? The man his children adored? The man every one of them wanted, more than anything in this world, to emulate?

Some would say later that it was one of the most impressive ceremonies in a city known for its pomp and ceremony. The long, long lines of men and women in blue, filling both sides of the street for miles. The mourners trailing the casket to the cemetery under a freezing drizzle. Gunshots echoing in the frigid air as the chief of police handed the flag to Riordan Lassiter's widow.

But when it was over, Micah would remember one thing most clearly. His grandfather, the strong, tough ex-cop who had survived gunshots, knife wounds and a gang shoot-out that had left him with a permanent limp and an early retirement from the police force, had broken down and wept like a child. That, more than any other moment, left the young boy with the hard knot of fear in the pit of his stomach. This wasn't just a bad dream. His father was truly gone. And from this day forward, Micah's life would be forever changed.

He bit down hard on the fear and made himself a promise. No matter what path he chose in life, it would be one of service to others. And no matter how tough the obstacles, he would stay the course until he became the sort of man that would make his father proud.

Washington, D.C., 1998

"Top Dog is on his way."

Word that the president was leaving the Mayflower Hotel after his luncheon speech quickly sped through the earphones of the Secret Service.

It was a perfect spring afternoon in the nation's capital. Thirty-year-old Micah Lassiter allowed his gaze to sweep the crowd of excited onlookers being held back while the president walked to his waiting limousine. Out of the corner of his eye he saw a man stretch out his hand. Sunlight glinted off steel. Micah's reaction was instantaneous. With his gun drawn, he shoved the president to the ground and knelt over him, taking the gunman down with a single bullet.

All around him were the sounds of screaming and shouting. Men cursed as they issued orders in staccato voices. Unharmed, the president was rushed to his limousine, surrounded by a wall of bodyguards.

Micah didn't feel the pain at first. Only an odd numbness. It was then that he realized he was lying on the sidewalk. He tried to get up, but his body refused to cooperate. As he touched a hand to his chest, he felt the sticky warmth of blood and knew he'd taken the bullet meant for the president.

"Don't move, Micah." Will Harding, whose prematurely white hair and military bearing gave him the look of a veteran, knelt beside his friend. "The ambulance is on the way."

Micah wanted to ask him about the shooter, but though his lips moved, no words came out. It occurred to Micah that the voices had begun to fade. As had the blur of faces peering down at him.

He was vaguely aware of being moved to a gurney and lifted into the back of the ambulance. Each tiny movement brought excruciating pain.

So this was how it felt to die. He'd always wondered just what his father had gone through. He could barely hear the sound of the sirens as they sped down the block. Everything sounded muted. As though filtered through a sea of mud.

By the time they reached the hospital, the pain was a searing hot flame, threatening to burn away his flesh and melt his bones.

His clothes were cut away, and doctors poked and prodded. There were questions. Too many questions. He was beyond caring about the answers now. When at last a needle was thrust into his arm, he felt himself slipping down until there was only darkness. He would welcome death if it would just end this vicious, clawing pain.

Micah lay perfectly still, wondering at the strange sounds. Beeps, blips, and a loud whooshing, like heavy breathing. An automatic blood-pressure cuff tightened at his arm, causing his eyes to flicker, then open.

"Praise heaven. Look, Katie girl, he's awake."

Micah recognized his grandfather's Irish brogue, and glanced over to see the old man standing beside his bed.

On the other side were his mother, his sister, Bren, and his brother, Cameron. The only one missing was Donovan, who was rumored to be somewhere in Central America.

"Not—" he struggled to make his mouth move "—dead, I guess."

"Not by a long shot, Micah my boy." Kieran Lassiter clamped a hand over his grandson's. "I told your mother you're a fighter."

Micah saw the tears in his mother's eyes. That hurt almost as much as the wound. "What's... damage?"

"You took a bullet to the chest." Kate Lassiter forced a smile. "Obviously it missed the heart, or you wouldn't be here talking to us."

"What else?" Micah looked beyond his mother to Cameron, who would, he knew, be brutally honest.

Cam glanced at the others before saying, "You have a collapsed lung, some broken ribs, some damage to the chest and left shoulder. The doctors think you'll be in here for a little while. You're going to need some therapy for that shoulder. But you'll be good as new in no time."

Micah closed his eyes, letting the words sink in. When he opened them, he saw the way his mother and grandfather were looking at each other. Obviously there were things they weren't telling him yet.

Before any of them could speak, there was a commotion outside the room, and the president, accompanied by the Secret Service, was striding toward Micah's bed.

The voice, so familiar to all Americans, sounded loud in the sudden silence. "I wanted to be here when you woke. Sorry I'm late."

Micah managed to smile, despite the pain. "You've got...a country to run."

"And thanks to you, I'm still here to run it." The president put a hand on Micah's shoulder. Squeezed. "I'll never forget what you did, Micah."

"Just doing my job, Mr. President."

"I understand. But there is nothing more humbling than to know that you're lying here in my place, Micah. For that, your president, and your country, are grateful." He glanced over and saw one of his aides tap a finger on his watch. "I'm afraid I have to run. I want you to do whatever the doctors tell you, Micah. And when you're out of here, I'll find a proper way to thank you."

With a retirement medal, Micah thought as the darkness closed in around him. Despite the drugs that had his mind clouded, his body numbed, he was still sharp enough to understand the seriousness of his wounds.

All the years of training, all the challenges, both mental and physical, had just come to an end with one shooter, one bullet. His dreams of spending a lifetime in service to his country as a Secret Service agent had just gone up in smoke.

But he knew, as he lay there drowning in pain, that if he were called upon to do it again, he would. Without a moment's hesitation.

Chapter 1

"Micah. Get your hands out of that bowl of strawberries. They're for dessert tonight." Bren Lassiter rapped her brother's knuckles with a wooden spoon.

"I only wanted a couple." With a devilish grin he popped a handful of juicy berries into his mouth before she could stop him.

"That's more than a couple. If you wanted to eat some, you should have offered to help clean them."

"And deny you the pleasure of your one domestic chore?"

''That's one more than I've seen you do lately. You've a nerve, dropping by Mom's just in time for dinner, and always managing to leave when it's time to clean up the kitchen.''

''That's right, Congresswoman. You tell him.'' Cameron, their youngest brother, who lived above the garage of their mother's big, sprawling home, ambled into the kitchen and opened the refrigerator, before lifting a carton of milk to his lips and chugging it down.

''That's disgusting.'' Bren put her hands on her hips. ''You'd think a man smart enough to graduate at the top of his law class would know better than to spread germs like that.''

''Germs?'' Cameron lowered the carton. ''Who says I have any?''

''If that tart I saw you cuddling up with in Farrell's last week was any indication of the type of women you're dating lately, I'd say you have plenty of germs to worry about.''

''At least I have someone to cuddle with, Congresswoman.'' Cam stashed the milk and leaned against the refrigerator door. Ever since his sister had been elected to her first term of Congress from the state of Maryland, he'd enjoyed her new nickname. ''How's your love life lately?''

His sister cuffed him on the side of the head

hard enough to see stars. "At least I don't put my love life on display at the neighborhood tavern."

"Oh, I'm betting you would. If you had a love life, that is. By the way, what're you doing visiting here tonight? Don't you have a committee meeting or something?"

"That's tomorrow night. And I thought I'd drop by so Mom wouldn't feel outnumbered by all you sweaty jocks."

"Sweat's a good thing." Micah winked at his brother. "Women love the smell of a locker room."

Bren made a sound of disgust. "What kind of women have you been hanging out with?"

"Obviously not any as interesting as Cam's." He leaned close to sneer. "A tart, huh?"

Cameron gave his older brother a hard, quick shove. "Who says?"

Micah good-naturedly shoved back. "Bren, for one."

Cameron's fist shot out, catching Micah on the shoulder. "And you'd take her word over mine?"

"As a matter of fact, I happened to be at Farrell's and saw for myself." Micah threw one quick punch that landed on the side of Cam's head. "I wouldn't exactly call her a tart. But I did think that if she sneezed, the entire tavern crowd would have seen more of her than the doctor who delivered her. Which couldn't have been more than seven-teen or eighteen years ago, if you ask me, cradle-robber.''

"Nobody asked you. And she's twenty-two.'' This time the punch thrown was harder, sending Micah back against the kitchen counter.

He straightened, and was just ready to retaliate when their grandfather came bustling into the kitchen, trailed by their mother, a petite redhead who looked barely older than her daughter. In fact, with their fiery hair and pale, Irish skin, they could have been twins.

Kieran Lassiter narrowed a gaze on the two men. "Outside to the hoops, the two of you.''

"We weren't...'' Cameron started to speak, then caught the blaze of fire in the old man's eyes.

Bren chuckled. "You'd think the two of them would grow up, Pop.''

"Grow up, is it?'' Cam glowered at his sister. "Seems to me you were the one to start all this with that smart-aleck remark.''

"All I said was your date looked like a tart.''

"Mary Brendan.'' Kate Lassiter always reverted to her daughter's full name whenever she was shocked or annoyed.

Cam was angry enough to spit nails. "You take that back, Bren, or I'll...''

"All right.'' Kieran Lassiter's eyes had turned

to ice-blue chips. His voice, which always carried a hint of a brogue, thickened with anger. "I said take it outside to the hoops. All three of you."

"But I—" Bren started to argue, then, seeing her mother's look, clamped her mouth shut and followed her two brothers out the back door.

As Micah picked up the basketball and started dribbling, she and Cam circled him.

Under her breath Bren muttered, "Almost thirty, and still being sent outside to work off my aggression. When does it end?"

"Probably when the next generation of Lassiters comes along, and it's our turn to give the orders." Micah easily broke away from their defense and made a basket before tossing it to his sister.

As he and Cam were circling her, the door opened and Kieran shouted, "Micah. Somebody here to see you."

"Tell them he's busy doing his punishment," Cam called as he slapped the ball out of his sister's hand and ran up for a layup.

The old man's voice sharpened. "The man says it's business, Micah. I don't think you want to keep him waiting."

"Yeah. Okay." Micah caught the ball as it slipped through the hoop, then tossed it to his sister. "This time hold on to it and play like a guy."

"That's the only way I know how to play." She

gave him a shove as he walked away, then turned to fend off Cam's advance.

On his way inside, Micah picked up a towel and mopped at his face before walking through the kitchen to the great room, where two men were standing just inside the door.

"Micah Lassiter?" A tall, rangy man dressed casually in a golf shirt and slacks strode across the room and stuck out his hand. "Allen Street."

"Mr. Street."

"I prefer Allen."

"Allen." Micah was taken aback by the casual clothing and the casual greeting.

Allen Street was one of the wealthiest men in the country. A surprisingly boyish-looking electronics whiz who had created the most successful computer software company in the world. He'd phoned earlier, requesting this meeting. When Micah had suggested going to his office in Bethesda, Allen Street had refused, requesting a more informal setting, where he wouldn't be recognized. When he'd also refused to meet at Micah's home just down the block, Micah realized that Street was taking no chances on being videotaped or recorded. He was known as a reclusive man who resisted the public eye. This place seemed a safe middle ground in which to meet. Especially since he'd arrived more than two hours earlier than planned.

Street turned to include the other man. "I believe you know Will Harding."

"Will, good to see you again." Micah offered his hand to his old friend. "I heard you'd left the government service to take a private security job. Until now, I didn't know where."

The man gave a slow easy grin. "Looks like it happens to all of us eventually. Allen made me an offer I couldn't refuse."

Micah pointed to a sofa and a pair of chairs set before a fireplace. "Why don't you two make yourselves comfortable. Coffee?"

"No, thanks." Allen Street dropped a thick manila folder into Micah's hand before settling himself in the chair. "I'd like you to take a look at these."

Micah opened the folder to reveal a packet of letters and e-mails. He picked up the first and read in silence. Then he read a second and third before looking up. "It's pretty obvious that these three are from the same writer. How about the rest?"

Street turned to Harding. "As far as we can determine, they're all from the same hand."

Micah tapped a finger on the page. "From the little I read, he seems to believe that the software package that came with his computer was programmed to spy on him. Is that about right?"

Street nodded. "He's convinced that his software is sending back intimate information about him to my company, and to me, personally. He claims to have been fired from a string of jobs because I fed his employers personal information about him. As you can imagine, in my line of work I've had to deal with a lot of crank letters. But my security team feels that this guy is different from all the rest. For one thing he's brilliant. Smart enough to break through my private computer code while concealing his identity. And from the tone of those letters and e-mails, he's definitely unbalanced and dangerous. He comes across as a man obsessed.''

Micah nodded. ''That sounds about right.'' He leaned back. ''So why are you here? What makes you think I can do something more than your own security team?''

''I have the best minds in the business working on tracking him. I have no doubt we'll eventually be successful. I've already arranged for around-the-clock security at my home in Seattle. My daughter is another matter, however. She's a graduate student in Georgetown. What I'd like to do is put her in a glass bubble and lock her away in a vault. But since she refuses to cooperate, I've decided on the next best thing. Until we can find this person and put my fears to rest, I want someone around her night and day to see that she's kept safe.''

Street leaned forward. The round glasses gave him an owlish appearance. His red-brown hair showed not a trace of gray. But his boyish looks were deceiving. Though he was known to be clear-headed and calm under fire from his competitors, at the moment it was obvious to Micah that this man was agitated and deeply troubled. And absolutely determined to protect his turf.

"Will tells me that you're the best in the business, Lassiter. Naturally I had you investigated thoroughly before coming here.''

If he'd hoped to catch Micah by surprise, he was disappointed. Micah smiled. "I'd expect no less. What did you find?''

"That you ranked highest in every area of the Secret Service.'' Street studied the man before him in the stained sweats. The body had been honed like a fine weapon. And the eyes seemed warm and friendly until you looked beneath the surface and saw the way they locked on a target like a laser. This was a man you didn't want to cross.

His voice lowered. "You deliberately took a bullet meant for the president. That isn't something just any man can do, Lassiter.''

"It is if you're part of the Secret Service. That's our job. Ask Will here.''

"Believe me, I have asked Will."

When he'd asked Will Harding to describe Micah Lassiter in one word, that word had been *lethal*. Micah had a reputation for finishing whatever he started, even if it meant facing down death.

"Your record shows that you went above and beyond duty, Lassiter. That injury forced you to give up the work you'd trained and sweated for. But instead of taking your disability pay and nursing your wounds, you started your own security company." He saw Micah open his mouth and lifted a hand to stop him. "A security company which is, by all accounts, after just a year in operation, considered the best there is. I know, too, that the kind of courage you displayed runs in your family. Over twenty years ago your father took a bullet meant for his partner."

He saw a quick look come and go in Micah's eyes and realized the pain of that loss was as fresh as if it had happened yesterday. "That tells me something about the integrity of the man I'm hoping to hire to protect my most precious treasure." He pushed at his glasses, magnifying the intensity of his gaze. "And make no mistake, Lassiter. My daughter, Prudence, is very dear to me. I'll do whatever it takes, pay whatever it costs, to keep her safe until this madman is caught and put away."

He sat back and rested his hands on his knees. "Will you take the job?"

Micah glanced at the pile of letters. "I'll want to read through all of these. Are they originals or copies?"

"Copies. The originals are with the FBI."

Micah nodded. "If the rest are as twisted as these, I'd say you're very wise to involve the FBI." He folded his hands atop the letters. "I'd be happy to assign an operative to tag along with your daughter until this is cleaned up."

Street was already shaking his head. "You don't understand. I don't want one of your operatives. I want you, Lassiter."

"That's very flattering, Allen, but I have an agency to run."

Street fixed him with a steely look. "You're the only one I'm willing to trust with my daughter's life."

Micah thought about all the reasons why he should refuse. But he recognized the desperation in this man's eyes and thought about his own family. If this were about his grandfather, his mother, his sister or brothers, he'd move heaven and earth to keep them safe.

He let out a quiet sigh. "All right. I'll see to her myself."

"Excellent." Street reached into his pocket and

produced a slip of paper. "This is where Prudence lives. I'll expect you to get to work immediately. The clock starts ticking now."

Micah accepted the paper, idly noting the exclusive address in Georgetown. "Consider it done."

"There's just one thing." Street was regarding him carefully. "You'll have to protect my daughter without her knowledge."

Micah looked at the man as if he couldn't believe what he'd just heard. "What possible reason could you have for not warning her about the danger she might be facing?"

"Living with the sort of notoriety my success has produced can be a difficult thing for a child. Especially one as painfully shy as Prudence. I'm sure it was aggravated by the fact that her mother died when Prudence was only three. I may have been a bit overly protective, but it was for her own good. At any rate, she insisted on moving as far away from home as possible while working on her degree. She seems to have found a certain amount of joy in being anonymous. If she thought I'd hired a bodyguard, she'd be furious with me."

"She has a right to know about the danger."

Street nodded. "And she will. When and if it's considered necessary for her safety. But for now, I don't want to alienate her any more than necessary. She's determined to live her life without re-

straint.'' He got to his feet and stuck out his hand.
''Is it a deal, Lassiter?''

Micah gave a reluctant nod. ''It's a deal, Allen.
I'll do my best.''

''I'm counting on it.''

As Street started to relax, Micah's tone hard-
ened. ''But make no mistake. If I feel your daughter is in harm's way, I'll demand that you tell her
the truth. If you don't, I will.''

''You have my word on it.'' Street handed him
a check. ''This should get you started.''

When he and Will Harding were gone, Micah
studied the amount of the check and gave a low
rumble of laughter.

As he pushed open the kitchen door he found
his entire family, including his mother, making an
effort to look busy.

''I suppose—'' he paused to dip a hand in the
bowl of strawberries ''—you're all going to pretend that you weren't standing with your ears
pressed to the door so you could overhear all
that?''

''All what?'' Kate Lassiter was busy slicing
bread.

''Don't try to look innocent, Katie girl.'' He
gave a fine imitation of his grandfather's brogue.
''My business arrangement with Harold Street.''

"Allen Street," Kieran Lassiter corrected. "And he doesn't look like a millionaire to me."

At that the others burst into laughter. "Micah got you this time, Pop."

Kieran glowered at his grandson. "So we were listening at the door." He added with a trace of pride, "There isn't much that gets by the Lassiter family."

Bren stepped closer. "So, how much was the check?"

Micah merely smiled and tucked the slip of paper in his pocket. "Let's just say it's enough to set me up in high style. Or enough to run off and buy myself a small country if I were so inclined."

"You aren't going to tell us?" Cam gave him a punch to the shoulder that had him spinning backward.

Micah turned around with both fists raised.

That was all their grandfather needed. "You'll take it out to the hoops until it's time for dinner."

As Micah and Cameron headed outside, Micah muttered, "I wonder if Pop would send Allen Street out back to work off his aggression?"

"Probably." Cam grinned. "And then for good measure he'd have him donating a fortune to the police retirement fund."

Chapter 2

"Ah. Here you are, my boy." A dapper gentleman in a navy blazer and crisp gray slacks looked up from the small cluster of people gathered around him and turned to Micah with a smile. "I was just telling my neighbors how lucky I was that you happened by when you did. The timing couldn't have been more perfect." He indicated the well-dressed couple to his left. "Randall and Helena Crispin, I'd like you to meet Micah Lassiter. Years ago, when Micah was in my class at Georgetown, he was my brightest student."

"Randall. Helena." Micah already knew all about them. As well as everyone else in this building. This was Randall's second marriage. His first, when he'd been in college, had lasted less than a year. He and Helena had been married for seventeen years now, and both worked for the State Department. Their records, which Micah had gone over with two of his operatives, were spotless.

"And these," the professor said with a smile, "are Octavia and Odelia Vandevere."

Micah had been looking forward to meeting these two elderly sisters. Their father had been a lawyer, and later a federal judge, who had amassed a fortune before his death. Though neither of his daughters ever married, they had been, sixty years ago, considered two of the most beautiful and eligible young socialites in the city. And though some might consider them a bit eccentric, Micah could find no reason to worry about their presence in the building, except as professional busybodies.

Micah offered a handshake to each of them. "Miss Vandevere. And Miss Vandevere."

Octavia, older by a year, touched her hand to her heart. "Oh my, Odelia. What a handsome, charming addition to our little family." She turned to include the young woman who held herself slightly apart from the others. "Wouldn't you agree, Prudence, dear?"

The young woman standing to one side turned several shades of pink.

Ignoring her young friend's embarrassment, the older woman couldn't resist pressing a bit more. "Micah Lassiter, do you have a wife and children?"

"No, ma'am. No wife and no children."

"Any angry ex's lurking in the bushes?"

He laughed. "No, ma'am. I'm an avowed bachelor."

"Well, now. Isn't that interesting, Odelia?"

Before the professor could finish the introductions, the two Vandevere sisters had completely taken over. "Come, Prudence, dear. Meet our new neighbor. Micah Lassiter, this is Prudence Street. Mr. Lassiter, if there's anything at all you want to know about the neighborhood, Prudence here is the one to ask. Isn't that right, Odelia?"

"Oh, indeed." Odelia's voice was as wispy as a child's. "Our Prudence is just the smartest little thing. Out and about every day. Walking. Driving her fancy little car. She knows just about everything."

"Is that so?" Micah turned to her with a smile. And though he'd had plenty of time to study photographs of Prudence Street, from infancy to her college graduation, the photos hadn't done her justice. He wasn't prepared for the pretty young woman with the small, heart-shaped face, amber eyes and windblown honey hair. Her cheeks were gloriously pink, as though she'd just come in from a brisk walk in the spring breeze. The tailored linen slacks and shirt were the color of ripe strawberries. Though her smile was shy, her handshake was firm enough.

"Mr. Lassiter."

"I prefer Micah. Do they call you Prudence or Pru?"

"Her friends call her Pru." Octavia wasn't about to allow her young friend's shyness to get in the way of a possible friendship or, even better, a possible romance. The wheels were already turning.

Pru lowered her gaze. But not before taking note of laughing blue eyes and a ruggedly handsome face. During their handshake she'd absorbed a jolt, and blamed it on the fact that she'd been caught unaware. Her hand was actually tingling from the brief contact with this man's. She hadn't expected to meet her new neighbor when she agreed to join the others in bidding the professor goodbye.

She turned toward her old neighbor. "Have a wonderful time in Europe, Professor Loring. I'll look forward to your many tales of adventure when you return."

"Not too many adventures at my age, I should hope." He gave a booming laugh. "But having this offer come right out of the blue is adventure enough. Here I thought I'd be spending a quiet summer in my garden with you, my dear.'' He squeezed Pru's hand. ''I hope you'll keep all my blooms in good health until I'm able to see them in September.''

''You can count on it, Professor Loring.''

The old man handed Micah a set of keys. ''This small one is the security key, to get in the front door of the building. This larger one opens the door of my apartment. I'm so grateful to you for offering to take over this place, Micah. Now I won't have to worry about a thing while I'm gone.''

Micah was listening with only half his mind. His eyes narrowed on Pru Street as she seemed to shrink from the others. It would appear that, though she'd boldly fled the confines of her father's mansion in Seattle, she hadn't completely shed her shyness. ''I'm happy to do it, Professor.''

''I still can't get over the timing of my young friend's visit.'' The professor turned to his neighbors. ''Why, I'd only just received the call about shepherding a class of students across Europe and was still reeling from all the details I would have to see to. And the next thing I knew, here was Micah, and I realized that I could now relax and enjoy myself, knowing all my possessions would be in his very capable hands. He's in security, you know. What could be more reassuring than to know I have my very own private security agent living in my place? Isn't that an amazing coincidence?''

If he only knew the truth, Micah thought. It was fascinating to see how many deals could be cut and red tape eliminated with enough money to be spread around. It had been a fairly simple matter to learn who lived in the apartment next to Prudence Street. From there a few phone calls were all it took to get rid of the professor for the summer in a way that would benefit the old man while affording Micah the proximity he needed to do his work. Micah had come up with several different stories he'd intended to run by the old man in order to be allowed to sublet the apartment. None of them had been necessary. The professor had managed his money wisely, and had no need of anything more than an assurance that his precious apartment and its luxurious appointments would be kept safe in his long absence. Who better than the head of a security company? The old man had leaped at the opportunity to have Micah live in his place for the summer.

''Would you like me to drive you to the airport, Professor?''

''No, indeed. One of my students who's traveling with me is picking me up.'' The old man looked up at the sight of a van pulling to the curb outside. "There he is now." He turned to his neighbors. "I'll say my goodbyes."

He was smothered in kisses by the Vandevere sisters, hugged by Helena Crispin and had his hand pumped firmly by her husband, Randall.

He leaned close to brush a peck on the cheek of Prudence Street. "Take care of yourself, my dear."

"You, too, Professor." She barely glanced at the man beside him, for fear she would blush again. "It was nice meeting you, Micah."

"Nice meeting you, too, neighbor."

The Vandevere sisters weren't through yet. Octavia slowed Pru's retreat with a hand on her arm. "You'll be certain to let Prudence know if you need anything, young man?"

To which Odelia chimed in, "I'm sure our Prudence would be happy to help you settle into our little family here."

"Thanks. I'll be sure to take you up on that." Micah couldn't help chuckling at the two old busybodies' obvious attempts at matchmaking.

The professor turned to him. "If you don't mind giving me a hand with the luggage, Micah, I'll be on my way to my grand summer adventure."

He lifted a small valise, leaving the larger pieces for Micah to carry and led the way outside.

Minutes later, Micah waved goodbye and

headed inside the apartment. As he looked around at the elegant marble surround of the fireplace and the leaded glass doors on the bookshelves, he shook his head. Not exactly the style he was accustomed to in his bachelor digs, but it was certainly luxurious. This once-exclusive town house had been converted into four apartments. Two on the upper level, and these two on the ground floor.

The upper tenants, the Crispins and the Vandevere sisters, shared a balcony and rooftop garden. The professor and Prudence Street shared a walled garden in the rear of the house that was already a riot of colorful blooms.

Prudence Street.

Micah had studied early photos of her that had revealed a paler, thinner version of her father, with owlish glasses and red-gold hair styled in a short bob with straggly bangs. Street had been right about one thing. His daughter had definitely changed her image since coming to Georgetown.

Micah couldn't help smiling at the transformation in his new neighbor. Not just in the way she looked, but in the way she struggled to overcome her shyness. Maybe she wasn't the boldest woman he'd ever met. But at least she hadn't bolted when the Vandevere sisters had offered her services in helping him settle in. And though they didn't know it yet, Octavia and Odelia had just given him the perfect window of opportunity.

He was humming as he began unpacking clothes and hanging them in the walk-in closet.

Pru's fingers moved easily over the keyboard. With the semester ended, she was looking forward to a more leisurely pace at Georgetown. She intended to take only one hour-long class during the summer months, giving her more time to spend working for a nearby charity. It was satisfying work that had come to mean a great deal to her.

She felt a quick flash of annoyance when the doorbell rang. Since the tenants were insulated from outside intrusion, she assumed it must be the building's superintendent.

She peered out. Seeing her new neighbor, she unlocked the door.

"Hello." At once she felt the jolt of that intense gaze and realized she hadn't imagined it the first time. Micah Lassiter had a way of looking at her that had the heat rushing to her cheeks. There was, behind those laughing blue eyes, an air of something deep and dark and calculating. An air of mystery that was intriguing.

"Hi, neighbor. I hope you don't mind, but I decided to take you up on the Vandevere sisters' offer."

"Offer?" She pushed at her glasses, which had dropped down her nose.

He saw the look of confusion and smiled. "They told me if I needed any help settling in to let you know."

"Oh. Is there something you need?"

"Yes. If it isn't too much trouble." He casually leaned a hand on the door. As he did, his fingers brushed hers in passing. The quick rush of heat managed to catch him by surprise.

At the contact he saw her take a step back. It would seem that the lady was cautious with strangers.

He managed an easy smile. "I was so busy moving my things in, I forgot to eat today. All of a sudden I realized I was starving, and didn't know of any restaurants in the area that might have takeout before it gets too late."

"Late?" She glanced over her shoulder and was surprised to see that the streetlights had come on.

"I see I'm not the only one who gets lost in work." His smile grew. "Tell you what. You give me the name of a good restaurant in the area, and I'll bring back enough for two."

She was already shaking her head and backing away. "That isn't necessary."

"I insist." Without waiting for an invitation, he took a step inside, keeping his smile at full voltage to put her at ease. "It's the least I can do for intruding."

When she hesitated a moment longer he pressed his advantage. "Anything will do. Chicken, ribs, pizza."

"Pizza." She couldn't help smiling. "You just said the magic word. I'll see what I can come up with." She turned away and headed toward the kitchen.

Micah studied a room that was identical in size to the one across the hall. But where the professor had surrounded himself with clutter from his past, Pru Street apparently liked things sunny, bright and airy. The walls of the foyer and great room were butter yellow. The carpet white. Just beyond the foyer the furniture was a comfortable mix of contemporary and traditional, with a high-backed sofa in a yellow-and-green plaid that looked cozy enough to sleep on, and two floral chairs that shared a fringed hassock.

Pru paused in the doorway of the kitchen. "There are two carryout restaurants within a couple of blocks. But only one that offers pizza."

"All right, then. That's the one we want."

She smiled as she walked toward him, holding out a menu. "You can look this over and see what you'd like to order. I can phone from here if you'd like. It will save you going back to your place."

"All right." He studied the menu a moment then said, "Since we both want pizza, let's share. What would you like on it?"

"Onions and green pepper. But only on half. You can have whatever you like on the other half."

"Fair enough. I'll have pepperoni and cheese."

As she picked up the phone he added, "And a salad and bread sticks."

She spoke into the phone, then disconnected and set it aside. "They said you can pick up your order in about twenty minutes. If you'd like, I could draw you a map to the restaurant."

He shook his head. "No need for that. Just tell me which way to go. I have a pretty keen sense of direction."

"All right. Suit yourself. It's two blocks east, then maybe half a block south. There's a dry-cleaning shop next door."

He nodded. "I'll find it. Thanks, neighbor."

As he turned and let himself out, Pru studied the closed door and found herself wondering what in the world had just happened. It wasn't like her to warm up to strangers. Especially tall, dark and handsome ones who looked entirely too sure of themselves.

Still, there was no denying that she liked his smile. Besides, Professor Loring had called Micah

Lassiter his brightest student. If that sweet old man was willing to trust Micah with his precious belongings for the next four months, she could certainly trust him enough to share a pizza with him.

She knew she ought to return her attention to her computer. There was no sense wasting the next half hour. But as she struggled to concentrate, she kept thinking about the man who had just left her apartment. There was something so appealing about him. Maybe it was the laughter she could see in those blue eyes. Or the way his smile made her heart flutter just a bit.

She touched her hands to her cheeks and felt the heat. What nonsense. It had to be caused by the silly suggestion of the Vandevere sisters. Those two old dears were always trying to add some romance to her life. As if she needed such foolishness.

Annoyed, she shut down her computer program and, needing something to occupy her mind, removed her glasses and inserted her contact lenses. Not for vanity's sake, she told herself as she made her way to the kitchen in search of plates and napkins. She just wanted an unobstructed view of her handsome neighbor.

Chapter 3

Pru hated the fact that she was watching the clock. But it had been nearly an hour now, and her neighbor still wasn't back. What could be taking so long? She should have drawn him a map. Didn't all guys think they could find their way through a maze? She remembered always asking her father to stop for directions. He might be a genius when it came to computers, but one wrong turn could leave Allen Street wandering around for hours.

At the knock on the door she hurried across the room and peered out before throwing the safety lock. Micah was standing there holding a pizza box and two bags.

"What's all this?"

"I thought pizza and salad called for something more. So I picked up a bottle of Chianti." He moved past her. "I hope you have a corkscrew. I didn't think to buy one."

"I have one somewhere." She took one of the bags from his hand and led the way to the kitchen.

He set his burden on the table before taking the time to look around. "This is a great-looking room."

She dimpled, and it was obvious that she wasn't accustomed to receiving compliments. "Thanks. I've been having fun with it. It's the first place I've lived that's all just mine."

"I like the bright colors. It would be hard to be gloomy in a place like this."

"That's why I did it. I wanted everything to be light and fun." She rummaged in a drawer and held up a corkscrew. "Here it is. I knew I had one somewhere."

When she turned she bumped into him. It was like hitting a solid wall. She'd never in her life felt a body so rock steady. He didn't move. Didn't even blink at the collision. She was so startled all she could do was grab hold of his arm. Which only made things worse. His entire arm seemed to be a mass of rippling muscle.

"You all right?" He closed his hands over her upper arms and held her a little away.

"Yes, I'm...fine." She felt the quick rush of heat at his touch. She glanced up, but couldn't tell from his shuttered look whether or not he'd felt it too. She took a quick step back and watched while he returned his attention to removing the cork. Then, needing something to do, she opened a cupboard and produced two wineglasses.

Micah used the few minutes while he turned the corkscrew and drew out the cork to sort through his unsettling feelings. All of his training had taught him to leave his emotions behind when dealing with a client. It didn't matter if they were saint or sinner, they deserved his undivided attention. Each one deserved to feel safe and secure. Never once had he allowed himself to be distracted from his mission by personal feelings. But right now, right this minute, he was feeling something that disturbed him more than he cared to admit.

He'd wanted, for that one split second when their bodies had come together, to hold her there for a moment longer. She looked so surprised, and so sweetly embarrassed by her clumsiness, that he'd longed to comfort her.

At least that's all he was willing to admit to. Still, there was the nagging little thought that it wasn't so much Prudence Street he was thinking about, but himself as well. That quick rush had sent the adrenaline pouring through his body. There may be some lingering effects from his old wound, but his body certainly hadn't forgotten how to react to a woman's touch.

"Here you go." Micah filled two glasses and handed one to her, before setting the other aside and opening a foam box brimming with salad. "Now, if you have two salad bowls, I'll divide this and we can begin the feast."

She reached into a cupboard and produced two crystal bowls, careful not to make another sudden turn. "Do you need dressing?"

He shook his head. "They sent along oil and vinegar. Will that do, or would you prefer something else?"

"That's fine." She took a sip of wine and glanced up. "Oh, this is good."

"I'm glad you like it." He paused to taste, wondering at the sudden warmth in the room. Could two bodies generate this much heat with one simple touch?

She stood watching as he began dividing the salad. "You're good at this."

He glanced up with a smile. "Arranging takeout? You bet. I don't know how I'd survive without it."

"You don't cook for yourself?"

"When I have time. Which isn't often these days. How about you?"

She shrugged. "Once in a while. I actually like to cook, but there just doesn't seem to be much time with my postgrad classes and my work."

"Where do you work?" Not that he didn't already know. But he wanted to keep her talking. It would be good for both of them. Besides, he liked the sound of her voice. There was a breathiness to it that he thought was probably nerves. The fact that it was also lower than most women's voices made it especially sexy.

"At a place called the Children's Village." She retrieved a basket to set the bread sticks in. "We try to place abused or abandoned children with loving foster parents. I can't really call it work since I don't get paid. I donate my services."

"You work with the children?"

She flushed. "I hope to one day." If she ever found the courage. "Right now I spend my time working with the computers."

"You must be good at it."

Again that shy shrug before she looked away. "Computers have always been easy for me."

Sensing her uneasiness, he quickly shifted gears. "The salads are ready. Why don't we nuke the pizza while we get started on these?"

She put the pizza in the microwave. When she

crossed the room Micah held her chair, and indulged in one quick touch of her hair before taking a seat across from her.

He didn't know what shocked him more. The fact that her hair was even softer than it looked, or the fact that he'd given in to something so unprofessional. He was here to protect her, not to form any personal bond. Still, he couldn't see the harm in a moment's gratification.

He broke a bread stick and tucked into his salad. "How long have you been living here in Georgetown?"

"It's almost a year now. How about you?"

"The District is home to me. My family lives not far from here."

She dipped a bread stick in olive oil and nibbled. "Do you have brothers or sisters?"

"Two brothers and a sister."

"So many." She arched an eyebrow. "Where do you fit in?"

"I'm the oldest. Then my brother Donovan, two years younger, and my sister, Bren. Cam is the youngest." Micah chuckled. "Just don't ever call him the baby."

"He doesn't like that?"

"My grandfather says Cam came into the world fighting, and he's been fighting ever since. I guess that's what happens when you're the youngest of four.''

"You have a grandfather." Without realizing it her eyes took on a dreamy look. "I always thought it would be fun to have grandparents. Do you see him often?"

"Every day. He lives with us."

"You're kidding." She studied him over the rim of her glass. "You live at home?"

"Down the block, actually. I bought the house when it went on the market a couple of years ago. But I may as well live at home. I'm there almost every day."

"And the rest of your family all lives there?"

He shook his head. "Bren has an apartment in Chevy Chase. But she may as well be living at home, too, since she's there as often as she's at her place. My brother Donovan is…out of the country. And Cam is hunting for a place of his own. Right now he has the apartment above the garage of my mother's house."

"And you gave up all that to stay at Professor Loring's."

"I don't mind. I could see that he was uncomfortable leaving his place empty for so long."

When the buzzer went off, Pru hurried across the room and returned with a steaming pizza. She slid two slices onto plates and handed one to Micah. "You haven't mentioned your father."

"He died when I was twelve."

Something in the way he said it had Pru glancing over before deciding that it wouldn't be wise to follow that with any more questions about him. Though she'd lost her own mother at an early age, she had almost no recollection of her. Except for certain moments, when she thought she could almost smell her. But that wasn't something she ever admitted to others. "And your mother?"

His smile was back as he dug into the pizza. "She went back to law school after my father's death and now works as an advocate for families. Come to think of it, you'd find you have a lot in common with her. You'd like her."

It was obvious that he did, too. "And your grandfather?"

"Kieran Lassiter. A tough ex-cop who moved in after my father died and became our den mother. He does the shopping, the cooking, the cleaning. He has the heart of a lion and the soul of a poet. When any of us had a problem in our younger days, we knew we could take it to Pop Kieran and he'd help us find a way to solve it. But we were never fooled by his domestic act. We always knew he was the toughest guy around. And still is."

"Sounds like a fascinating family." She rested

her chin on her hands. "I don't think I'd know what to do with so many people around."

"You'd learn how to eat fast before the food was all gone." He glanced at the half-eaten slice of pizza on her plate as he reached for a second one. "And you'd learn how to crank up your voice a notch so you could be heard above the din."

She couldn't help laughing.

"How about you, Pru? Any brothers or sisters?" Though he knew the answer, he was curious to see how much she was willing to reveal about herself.

"No. I'm an only. At least that's how it's referred to in psychology classes."

"An only? Must be nice being the center of your parents' universe."

"I don't have parents. Just a father."

"And does he dote on you?"

"You could say that. A bit too much for comfort." She paused, amazed that she'd revealed something so personal to a man she'd just met.

Micah glanced over. "He's holding on a bit too tightly?"

"Something like that." She shrugged, then decided to throw caution to the wind. "He's smothering me. He doesn't know how to let go. I don't doubt that he loves me. It's just that sometimes he focuses too much attention on me. When you're an only, there's a lot of pressure. To please. To succeed. To make him proud of me. And it can be lonely, too. I often thought it would be fun to have a sister to share secrets with. Or a big brother to take on the world when it got to be too much for me to handle.''

Micah chuckled. ''You might want to talk to my sister about that. I'd be willing to bet that there are plenty of times Bren would happily trade three bullheaded brothers for a chance to be an only.''

''How about you, Micah? Did you ever resent having to share your parents with so many others?''

He sat back, sipping his wine. ''My mother claims that when she brought Donovan home from the hospital, I told her to take him back. But what did I know? I was only two. Still, even now there are times when he's a royal pain.''

He reached for a third slice of pizza and noted that she was still on her first piece. ''You'd definitely have trouble surviving the Lassiter clan.''

She laughed and polished off the last bite before picking up her wineglass. ''There are entire days when I forget to eat.''

''Entire...?'' He shook his head as he topped off her glass and then his own. ''As much as I enjoy my work, I can't say I ever forget about eating.''

''It just isn't one of my priorities.'' She shot him

a quick glance before looking down. "Professor Loring said you're into security. What does that mean?"

He shrugged. "I keep people, places, things safe."

She looked up. "You mean safe from theft?"

He nodded. "Or safe from whatever threatens harm."

She had a sudden thought. "Do you carry a gun?"

"When I have to."

She set down her glass. Something flickered in her eyes. "Are you carrying one now?"

"No."

She visibly relaxed.

He quickly changed the subject by indicating the half-eaten pizza. "Want any more of this?"

She shook her head.

"Let's wrap it and put it in your freezer for the next time you forget to eat."

She pushed away from the table and returned with some freezer wrap. While she wrapped and stored the slices, Micah cleared the table and handed her the half-empty bottle of wine. "You may as well save this, too. It'll go well with the leftover pizza."

She turned to him with a shy smile. "I'm glad you reminded me to eat. Right about now I'd probably be shutting down my computer and prowling the cupboards looking for something to hold back the hunger.''

"Happy to oblige, ma'am.'' He started out of the kitchen, with Pru following.

At the door he paused and turned to face her. "Thanks for the hospitality, neighbor. Next time we'll make it my placc.''

She kept her hands folded primly in front of her. "What do you think of Professor Loring's apartment?''

"It's certainly different. I especially like the shrunken heads on the library shelf.''

She couldn't hold back the laughter. "Those aren't shrunken heads. They're authentic masks he picked up on a trip to Ethiopia fifty years ago.''

Micah grinned. "That's a relief. I'll sleep much better tonight knowing that.''

Pru's laughter was as musical as the tinkling of a bell. "I think you're having fun with me.''

"Maybe just a bit.'' He touched a hand to her shoulder and saw her head come up sharply. He deliberately kept his tone light. "It's been fun, Pru. Thanks again.'' He withdrew his hand and yanked the door open. When he stepped into the hallway, he turned. "Good night.''

"Good night.'' She waited until he'd let himself into the apartment across the hall before closing her door and bolting it. Then she turned around and crossed her arms over her chest.

She'd experienced the most amazing rush of heat when he'd touched her. In fact, the warmth was still there, mocking her. What was worse, she was practically trembling.

It was the thought of that muscled body pressed to hers. Though it had all happened in an instant, she couldn't get it out of her mind.

She pushed away from the door. As she walked through her apartment it occurred to her that she'd had a grand time tonight. Doing nothing more than chatting with her new neighbor.

This was the first time she'd entertained a man in her apartment. Not that it was a date, or anything even remotely resembling one. But still, she had to admit she wouldn't mind doing it again.

Earlier today she'd resented the Vandevere sisters' intrusion into her private life. But right about now she wanted to kiss those two old sweethearts.

She stopped dead in her tracks. Or maybe what she really wanted was to kiss Micah Lassiter.

He had a wonderful face. Rugged and handsome, and a bit dangerous-looking. The danger seemed magnified now that she knew he sometimes carried a gun. She'd always thought that men who handled weapons were somehow barbaric. Still, there were those laughing blue eyes.

He was definitely a fascinating addition to the neighborhood.

In the apartment across the hall Micah was whistling as he fixed himself a cup of instant coffee. The evening had gone even better than he'd hoped.

He'd had a chance to see a little of Prudence Street's apartment. Enough to know that the layout was exactly like this. Which meant that he'd have no trouble figuring out any places that might afford an intruder easy entrance. What's more, he'd had a chance to observe her in her own space. She was naturally cautious, which would make his job a little easier. She wouldn't be careless enough to let a stranger into her apartment. Even expecting him, she'd checked through the peephole before unlocking the door.

After all he'd read about her background, he thought he knew this woman he'd been hired to protect. He knew that until the age of thirteen, she'd been taught at home by tutors. That she'd attended an exclusive girls' school, where she'd excelled in language and history. She'd been considered something of a loner in her small, local university. And she'd surprised everyone, including her father, when she'd insisted on leaving home for her graduate studies.

But the woman he'd met tonight had managed

to catch him by surprise more than once. For one thing, despite her privileged childhood, she seemed to have chosen to live a fairly simple lifestyle. Though it was true that this section of Georgetown was definitely the high-rent district, she lived without frills. No live-in help of any kind. According to his notes, she employed only a two-person cleaning team that attended to her apartment every Thursday, from ten in the morning until two o'clock in the afternoon. They'd been with her for the past year, and the agency that employed them had impeccable references.

He'd already had time to examine her car, parked beside his in the garage. A candy-apple-red sports car with all the bells and whistles. Unfortunately, even in the thickest traffic jam, it would make her an easy mark.

Another thing that surprised him was Pru herself. Knowing how shy she was, he'd expected her to be aloof. Restrained. And probably without much humor. Instead, she'd come across as sweet and funny. And though she held him at arm's length, she wasn't so much shy as cautious.

Cautious. That trait could hold her in good stead in the days to come. He hoped she would remain that way, at least until the FBI put this latest nutcase out of commission.

But along with being cautious, she was also a

creature of habit. He'd already studied her daily activities and found, to his dismay, that he could almost pinpoint her whereabouts to the minute. If he could, so could anyone stalking her.

He had his work cut out for him. He was going to have to stick to Prudence Street like glue until this was over.

And if it killed him, he was going to have to put that little collision out of his mind. The thought of the way she'd felt pressed against him still had the ability to grab him by the heart. Not a good thing when he was being paid to see to her safety.

He'd need to remind himself often that he'd been hired as her bodyguard. Not her lover.

Chapter 4

Pru checked the Monday morning weather forecast. Even though the morning was mild and the sky bright with sunshine, she decided to take along a raincoat and umbrella for the expected late-afternoon showers. She didn't mind the rain, as long as it didn't turn into a full-blown storm. She was absolutely terrified of storms.

She grabbed her purse and car keys and hurried out to the garage. The space beside hers was vacant. Her new neighbor, it would appear, had already left for work.

She frowned as she turned the key in the ignition and backed out. She'd spent far too much time last night thinking about Micah Lassiter. Now it was time to clear her mind and get ready for a new day.

She drove the few blocks to the Children's Village and parked, then walked next door to the Java Café for her morning coffee. When she spotted someone already sitting at her favorite outdoor spot, she felt a quick wave of annoyance. Then, as recognition dawned, she blinked in surprise.

"'Morning, neighbor." Micah got to his feet. "I was just having a morning cup. Care to join me?"

"I… Yes, thanks. I'll just go inside and order it."

He nearly laughed at the look on her face. She was as open as a book. He could read annoyance, which gradually turned to surprise and then acceptance. "No need. Mindy will be right out with mine." He glanced toward the door and saw the waitress heading their way. "Here she is now."

He held a chair and had a chance to admire the pretty picture Pru made in her prim office attire. A lemon-yellow skirt just skimmed her knees. The long matching jacket was made even brighter by a red silk shirt. She was as colorful as the flowers in her garden.

Pru sat down before greeting the young girl who'd been serving her coffee every morning since she'd discovered this place. "Good morning, Mindy."

"'Morning, Pru. The usual?"

"Yes, please."

"I'll be right back." The waitress gave Micah her best smile and a slow sideways glance as she set down his coffee before turning away.

He sipped, then sighed with pleasure. "Now that's coffee."

Pru tried not to stare at the ripple of muscles in his arm as he set down the cup. No wonder Mindy was giving him a second look. What woman wouldn't? There was just something about him that turned heads. "How did you hear about this place?"

"It may have been Randall Crispin." He was grateful when the young waitress returned with Pru's coffee, distracting her from asking any more questions.

"Here you are, Pru. Double cream, one sugar."

"Thanks, Mindy."

Again Pru noticed the waitress glance Micah's way before walking to another table for their order. She nudged aside a quick frown and took several long sips before sitting back to relax. "I look forward to this at the start of my day."

"I know what you mean." He indicated the series of low buildings next door. "So that's where you work."

"Yes. What about you? Are you doing work in the neighborhood?"

"As a matter of fact, I am. When I got back to my apartment last night there was a call from my service. Your boss wants me to take a look at the security."

She nearly bobbled her cup before setting it down. She glanced at him across the table. "You're going to be working at the Children's Village?"

He shrugged. "Just until I find out what's wrong with the system and get it operating properly."

It occurred to Pru that her pulse had just gone up several notches. Foolish, she knew, but there it was. And all because Micah Lassiter would be working nearby.

She finished her coffee. While she was still digging in her purse, Micah had already paid for their coffees and dropped some money on the table for a tip.

"Come on." He paused beside her chair. "You can show me around."

"All right." She led the way around a high fence to a locked gate. After she passed a card through a slot, the gate opened, and she and Micah stepped inside.

He paused as the gate swung closed. "Is this always locked?"

She shook her head. "Only from closing time until the first employees arrive in the morning. After that it remains unlocked to accommodate visitors and deliveries."

They crossed a courtyard and paused at the door to a one-story glass-and-brick building. Again Pru passed her card through the lock and pulled the door open.

Micah caught the door and held it while she walked in and glanced at the security panel. Seeing that it wasn't on she shrugged. "I guess someone came in ahead of us."

His gaze swept the entrance as she moved ahead of him and gave a running commentary. "This entire complex was donated by the Dumont family. Originally it was an orphanage and private school. Then dorms were opened for unwed mothers. As times changed, the orphanage and school were closed, and the agency began accepting children from broken or abusive homes. This part of the village is new. This houses the reception area and offices. Deliveries are made here. Unless they're too large. Then they're made at a loading dock that can only be reached on the next street. The staff offices are back here." She moved briskly along a hallway, pointing out the various closed doors.

"We have caseworkers, who work with the families of the children brought here. There are psychologists, psychiatrists, pediatricians and nurses, all of them volunteers." She stopped in front of a closed door and turned the knob before stepping inside. "And this is where I work."

Micah glanced at the cramped office, barely big enough for a desk, a chair and the wall of file drawers and cabinets. "What do you do?"

She opened a drawer and stashed her purse, before frowning at the pile of new folders tossed carelessly across her desk over the weekend. "I make sure that everything gets entered into a computer file. The child, his family, the type of behavior that necessitated bringing him here, the names of caseworkers or police agencies involved, any immunization records that might help determine if the child has serious medical problems, and finally, the names of any foster families that might be able to fill the special needs of each child."

Micah studied the bulging files littering her desktop. "Sounds like a lot of work."

She shook her head. "Mine is the easy job. All I have to do is deal with facts and figures and put them into a computer. Think about the doctors and nurses and caseworkers. They have to deal with the broken bodies, broken hearts and broken dreams of innocent children. I don't have the courage to do what they do.''

Micah gave a quick shrug of his shoulders. ''Oh, I don't know about that. You're here, Pru. Volunteering your time for the sake of those kids, when you could be out in the corporate world earning a big salary. That takes a certain kind of courage. It's something to be proud of.''

She knew she was blushing, but she couldn't help it. She felt such a glow of pleasure at his words. So many of her friends didn't understand what she was doing, volunteering her time in a small charity. They'd made no secret of the fact that they thought she was wasting her time and talent. Especially considering her family connections.

He turned when the door opened and saw a pretty, dark-haired woman standing in the doorway. She wore a navy suit with a name tag pinned to her lapel.

Pru easily handled the introductions. ''Micah Lassiter, this is the director of the Children's Village, Margot Jamison.''

''Ms. Jamison.'' He offered a handshake.

''Mr. Lassiter. Thank you for being so prompt.'' She glanced at Pru. ''I'll be back later. Right now I'd like to show Mr. Lassiter our security system.''

As he exited Pru's office, Micah turned and winked.

She wondered at the way her heart seemed to take a sudden quick bounce. Then, ashamed that she was behaving like a love-struck teen, she opened the first file folder and buried herself in her work.

Micah removed a metal plate from the wall and peered at the maze of colored wires. "This might take a while."

Margot Jamison looked over his shoulder with an impatient frown. "I don't care how long it takes, Mr. Lassiter. Just so you get everything up and running smoothly. When one of my staff phoned me last night to say the system was malfunctioning, I found your card in my file with the notation that you were the best in the business. Since this is a fairly old system, the company that installed it is no longer in the business."

"That's not a problem. I'm glad you called. I'll do what I can."

She turned away. "I'll leave you to your work. My office is at the end of the hall. Drop by when you're finished."

He nodded and waited until she was gone before attaching two simple wires. At once the lights on the unit began flashing. Moments later the monitor lights turned green, announcing that the unit was armed and ready to be activated.

Humming as he worked, Micah disconnected the wires once more and watched as the lights flickered, then faded. He had no intention of finishing his work so easily. Of course, he wouldn't bill the Children's Village for his hours. Especially since he'd been the one to disarm the unit in the first place. But he needed an excuse to stay close to Prudence Street. What better way than this?

He replaced the metal plate and decided it was time to take a closer look around the place where Prudence spent so many hours each day.

As he moved from the main office building to the activity center, he noted a dozen different places where a prowler could lurk without calling attention to himself. This was, after all, a public place. In order to accommodate the many professional people who worked or visited here, it had to be accessible during business hours.

Not the optimum situation for guarding someone's life. But then, he'd faced a lot worse.

He began making notes of the most obvious places, with ideas on how to make them safer while remaining open to the public. A few well-placed security cameras would help, and perhaps one of his operatives added to the staff for observation until this threat was lifted.

He headed toward Margot Jamison's office. It would be a whole lot easier if Allen Street would just allow him to be honest and open about this threat. But until Street gave his approval, Micah would just have to bluff his way through and see what came of it.

"As far as I can see, the security system should be operating at full capacity in a few days." Micah sat across from Margot, pausing every few minutes while she answered her phone.

"Sorry." She returned the phone's receiver to the cradle and sat back for the third time. "Some days are just busier than others." She managed a tired smile. "There are days when I feel like a juggler with too many balls in the air."

He nodded. "I don't want this to sound complicated. But I think, considering the number of children involved in this operation, you ought to consider tightening your security a bit."

"Tightening our security? Why, Mr. Lassiter? Do you think there's a danger?"

"There's always a danger when you're dealing with dysfunctional families. There could be an angry parent who feels that your agency is about to take his children away from him. Or one who fears jail because of what the authorities have found in the home."

"None of that has anything to do with us. We simply try to find shelter for abused or neglected children. And help for their families."

Micah held up a hand. "Sometimes even the best intentions can backfire. I'd like to draw up a map with a list of your most vulnerable areas, and a few options you might want to consider. There'll be no charge, of course. It'll just be an estimate of things you can do to protect your staff and the children who come here."

She sighed. "Thank you. I'd be happy to look at it. I don't mean to sound ungrateful. It's just that I have so much on my plate."

"I understand." He got easily to his feet and started toward the door. "I'll come by your office tomorrow with something you can study."

Minutes later, as he headed toward Pru's office, he saw the director of Children's Village walking to her car.

He paused in the doorway and studied Pru at the computer, her fingers flying over the keyboard.

"I don't think I've ever seen anyone type that fast."

Her head came up. The little frown on her face eased into a smile. "I've been playing on a computer since I was big enough to sit at the keyboard. How about you? Don't you have reports to write? Or do you have a secretary for that?"

He stepped inside and settled himself beside her desk. "No secretary. Just an assistant. But she makes me file my own reports. And my typing is pathetic. It's more the hunt-and-peck style." He nodded toward the flashing cursor on her monitor. "You almost ready to call it a day?"

She nodded. "This is the last file of the day. How about you? Is our security system up and running?"

"Yeah. Such as it is. If you're leaving soon I'll wait for you. We can walk out together."

"All right." She turned away to hide the pleasure she knew would be visible in her eyes.

Micah watched as she efficiently backed up the file to disk, then placed the folder in a cabinet before shutting down her computer.

She opened a drawer and retrieved her purse. As they walked outside, she glanced around. "Where's your car?"

"Parked over there." He pointed to a row of cars behind hers. "You go ahead. I'll follow you home."

As Pru climbed into her sports car and revved the engine, she saw Micah stepping into a dark sedan with tinted windows. Once inside he became invisible.

It occurred to her that the car definitely suited the man. Solid, but with a hint of the mysterious.

Chapter 5

Micah pulled his car into the garage beside Pru's. They'd navigated the traffic and made it home just as dusk was beginning to take over the city.

He held her door as she climbed out. When she brushed against him, he felt the quick sizzle of heat and struggled to ignore it.

"Do you have any plans for dinner?"

She shook her head, sending her hair dancing. "None. But I was thinking on the way home that I just might heat up that leftover pizza."

"We can do better than that." He hadn't given a thought to dinner until this very minute. But the touch of her made him realize that he wasn't ready to say good-night just yet. "Do you have a favorite restaurant in Georgetown?"

She thought a minute before nodding. "A couple. There's a Chinese place, a Greek restaurant and a little French bistro that features an outdoor café when the weather permits."

"Sounds like just the spot." He'd noticed the way her eyes lit when she'd mentioned it. "Let's try the French cooking." He nodded toward the stairs. "Why don't we change into something comfortable first?"

At her murmur of approval, he followed her from the garage.

At her doorway Micah paused. "I'll stop by for you in an hour. Is that enough time?"

"More than enough. I'll be ready." It wasn't until Pru had stepped inside her apartment and leaned against the door that she realized he'd done it again. With almost no effort at all on his part, he'd persuaded her to spend the evening with him.

Not that she objected. In fact, she found herself looking forward to it.

She danced across the room, unbuttoning her jacket as she did. An hour gave her time to shower and try on at least three outfits before he knocked on her door.

Pru's bed was littered with slacks and tops, long cotton skirts and simple springtime dresses. All of them discarded in haste after one look at herself in the full-length mirror.

She'd finally settled on simple flax-colored slacks and top with a heather-toned sweater tossed carelessly over her shoulders. Her hair was left long and loose, her face free of makeup.

When Micah knocked, she was ready. After a quick look through the peephole, she threw the dead bolt and opened the door.

"Right on time." He shot her a dangerous smile as he stood back, allowing her to step into the hall-way and lock the door.

"It would be pretty difficult to be late when you live just across the hall." She pocketed her key and started walking beside him. When she realized he was heading toward the garage, she stopped him with a hand to his arm.

She felt him tense as he stopped abruptly and turned to her. "What's wrong?"

"I thought we'd walk. It's only a few blocks from here."

"Walk?" His eyes narrowed slightly and he seemed to be considering the implications before giving a reluctant nod of his head and turning to-ward the front of the building.

He walked out ahead of her and paused a mo-ment before stepping aside and holding the door for her.

In that brief moment she had the strangest sensation that he'd been studying their surroundings, much the way a bank robber might survey the scene before stepping up to the teller. What nonsense. She shrugged aside the feeling.

When they started along the sidewalk, she gave him an admiring glance.

Drops of water still glistened in his dark hair from his shower. He was wearing charcoal slacks and a black cotton crewneck. He was, she realized, as easy to look at as he was easy to be with.

She flushed when he caught her looking at him, and needing something to say, blurted, "You look like you work out."

"I do."

"Every day?"

He nodded. "How about you, Prudence?"

She shrugged. "I've tried from time to time. But I guess that's the problem. Time. I never seem to have enough of it."

"Yeah. I know what you mean. That's what stops most people from getting into a regimen of exercise. Mine's probably more like a compulsion."

"Why?"

"My line of work, I suppose."

When they came to a crosswalk he casually brought a hand to her elbow and kept it there as they crossed the street.

Once again she was forced to absorb the shock of his touch. But she had to admit that it wasn't an altogether unpleasant sensation. Especially when he kept his hand there and continued walking beside her. With each step, she could feel the heat growing.

Suddenly a car's headlights flashed in their eyes and there was the sound of tires screeching. Pru's reaction was to freeze in midstride. Micah's was a far different reaction. He didn't flinch as, in one smooth motion, he drew her behind him and turned to face the unknown.

The transformation in him was amazing. Though he'd gone deadly still, he seemed poised to take on whatever came toward him, even if it proved to be a car hurtling through the air straight toward him.

In that instant she imagined him, like a super-hero, catching the car in his hands and tossing it aside as though it weighed no more than a feather.

The driver brought the speeding car under control and turned down a side street. In the silence, Micah mentally shifted gears and once again caught her arm. "Crazy driver."

Pru touched a hand to her heart. "Scared the daylights out of me."

He dropped an arm around her shoulders and could feel her trembling. "It's a good thing we're almost there."

"How would you know that?" She looked up at him. "Have you been here before?"

"No. But I looked it up before leaving the apartment."

That brought a smile to Pru's lips. "Don't you ever leave anything to chance?"

"Not if I can avoid it."

She was still grinning as they rounded a corner and caught sight of Café Paris. Lights had been strung in the trees and shrubs, offering a warm welcome. In a small courtyard were tables with white cloths and flickering candles. Inside it resembled a French bistro, with waiters in starched white shirts and black pants balancing trays laden with bottles of wine and covered dishes snaking their way between crowded tables.

Micah turned to Pru. "What's your choice? Indoors or out?"

She glanced around. "Outside if there's a table available."

Micah spoke with the maître d'. Minutes later they were led to a table in a quiet corner of the courtyard.

When a waiter approached, Micah picked up the menu. "Would you care for some wine?"

Pru nodded. Within a short time the waiter returned and filled two stemmed glasses with pale white wine before discreetly leaving them alone.

Pru sipped her wine and seemed to hesitate before asking, "Why were you reluctant to walk here?"

Micah shrugged. "There can be a lot of dangers out on the street."

"You mean like that car we heard?"

"Not exactly. Even riding in a car is no guarantee you'll survive being hit by a driver who's out of control. But walking, especially after dark, leaves you open to all sorts of other dangers."

"I suppose, because of the sort of work you're in, you're more aware of the dangers than the rest of us."

"Yeah. I guess that's true." He managed a smile and deftly changed the subject. "What do you feel like eating?"

"I've been thinking about it all the way here." When she wasn't thinking about Micah Lassiter, she thought with a flush. "The specialty of the house is a beef bourguignonne made with brandy and burgundy that may be the best in the world."

His smile grew as the waiter approached. "You've just made my choice easy."

He gave their order, then leaned back. He'd already studied the faces of everyone seated nearby, and none of them had sounded any alarm bells in his mind. He decided to relax and allow himself to enjoy the moment.

"What's that smile about?" Pru was running her index finger around and around the rim of her glass.

"It's about the place. This was a good choice. And about the night. It's just about perfect. And the company. Also perfect, I might add."

He saw the way her cheeks colored. It was so endearing. It was a good thing he hadn't mentioned just how lovely she looked by candlelight. That would have had her face flaming.

"I'm glad you like it. At first I started coming here because it was close to home, and I wasn't comfortable roaming too far until I got more familiar with the town. But then I decided that I liked coming back to the same place time and again." She ducked her head when she saw him studying her. "I suppose that exposes my timid nature."

"I don't see you as timid, Pru."

"You don't?" Her head came up and she forced herself to meet his direct gaze.

"No." He caught her fingers that kept worrying the stem of her glass. Held them when she tried to pull away. "A timid person wouldn't settle into an apartment all alone in a new town. Would you like to know what I see when I look at you?''

"I'm...not sure. Is it good or bad?''

He couldn't help chuckling. "I see a bright woman pursuing her doctorate at a very good university. A sweet, generous woman who donates her time to a worthy charity, when she could be doing a million other things. Like lunching with her friends. Or shopping.''

She shook her head. "I hate shopping.''

He gave a look of pretend shock. "What's this? Can it be true? A woman who hates to shop? If the word gets out, scientists will want to clone you. Men will want to nominate you for sainthood. Women will want you put out of your misery.''

Her laughter was a warm, musical sound in the night air.

They were both still laughing when the waiter brought their meal.

At his first taste, Micah paused, closed his eyes and gave a sigh of pure pleasure. "Now that's something I'd walk miles for.'' After that, he dug into his food.

"I'm glad you approve.'' Pru nibbled the garlic potatoes and found herself enjoying the way Micah seemed to savor everything with such zeal.

He glanced up. "Have you ever brought any of your co-workers here?''

She shook her head. "They all have families to go home to. Most of them are so busy, I often wonder how they find time for all the people who depend on them."

"Margot Jamison mentioned that she felt like a juggler with too many balls in the air."

"Exactly." Pru nodded. "I'm in awe of all the people who manage work, home, family responsibilities and the dozens of demands made on their time. When do they ever find time for themselves?"

Micah grinned. "Remind me to ask my mother." He glanced up when the waiter returned. "Coffee?"

Pru thought a moment. "Espresso, I think."

Micah turned to the waiter. "Make it two. And a crème brûlé with two spoons."

When the waiter returned with their dessert Micah winked at her across the table. "Now if you really want to live dangerously, I dare you to try to take just one bite."

"Unfortunately, I know what you mean. It happens to be my favorite dessert."

She dipped a spoon into the creamy confection and tasted, then gave a sigh of pleasure and helped herself to a second taste before moving it closer to him.

He took a bite, then another, before passing the

dessert back to her. Leaning back, he sipped his espresso and enjoyed her look of pleasure.

She had the most expressive face. He didn't think it would be possible for Prudence Street to keep a secret.

Maybe it was just as well that her father hadn't revealed the threat to her. It would be a shame to deny her such an innocent pleasure as this.

They sat for almost another hour, sipping coffee, watching the parade of patrons come and go. Finally he settled the bill and caught her hand. When they reached the sidewalk and started home, she was surprised when he kept her hand tucked in his.

In the darkness his voice sounded deeper, richer. "I remember always loving the springtime when I was a kid. You could see each day growing longer. That meant more time to toss hoops out in the driveway."

"You and your brothers played basketball?"

"And my sister, Bren. She couldn't help being a tomboy with three brothers. The minute we'd start roughhousing indoors, my grandfather would send us outside to work off our aggression on the basketball hoop."

"Did it help?"

He chuckled. "I'd hate to tally the number of times we bloodied each other."

She looked startled. "You fought?"

"Like cats and dogs." His grin widened. "I can see that you've led a very sheltered life. You haven't lived until you've humbled a mouthy kid sister, or given your brother a shiner."

"Did they ever get even?"

"You bet. That's the name of the game. I've had to take my share of bruises. Especially when they decided to gang up on me. But Pop was a very wise man. He knew we'd be able to leave our anger outside. At least until the next time, when he'd send us out to butt heads again."

"You make it sound like a family of goats."

"I think he'd agree with that." Micah laughed. "Or maybe a family of mules. Pop always says we're the most hardheaded bunch he's ever known. And it takes one to know one."

Pru heard the note of affection in his tone. "Despite what you've just described, I'd bet good money that the Lassiter family is short on temper and long on love."

"Long on love. Definitely. But the only thing short about our tempers is the fuse. We still head out to the hoops after dinner if we have to settle a hot political argument. Which happens at least once a week."

He walked with her up the steps to their apartment building and held the door.

Once inside, they walked together to the door of

Pru's apartment. She unlocked her door, punched the code on her alarm and paused in the doorway.

"Thanks for dinner, Micah." Her smile was radiant. "I had a great time."

"So did I." It was true. She was so easy to be with. With Prudence Street there was no artifice. Nothing contrived. And though he hadn't intended to touch her, he found himself running his hands across the tops of her arms as he stared down into those laughing eyes. "In fact, this has been one of the best and most relaxing nights I can remember."

He was studying her closely. "You have the most beautiful eyes."

She blushed. "It's the contact lenses."

He shook his head. "They say the eyes are the mirror of the soul. If that's true, you have one beautiful soul, Pru."

It seemed the most natural thing in the world to lower his face to hers. To brush his mouth over hers. He'd intended it to be no more than a simple good-night kiss. But the moment their lips met, everything changed.

He'd taken blows to the body before. Whether from fists or clubs or both. And he certainly knew how it felt to be flattened by a bullet to the chest. It was all part of the job. But he'd never before believed he could feel that same reaction from a simple kiss.

But then there was nothing simple about it. Her mouth was the softest, sweetest confection he'd ever tasted. Prudence Street put the dessert they'd shared to shame. And her body fit against his like the missing piece to a puzzle.

He was fully into the kiss before he realized what was happening. And by then it was too late to escape. He could feel himself sinking into her. Into all that sweetness. And losing himself completely in her, his head spinning, his heart doing a crazy dance in his chest.

Pru started to pull back, but she was held as surely as if she'd been planted in concrete. And then it was too late to resist. Her arms curved ever so slowly around his neck as she offered him more. The purring sound that came from her throat was as much a surprise to her as to him. And then, as he took the kiss deeper, she hung on, feeling her world begin to tilt and sway.

She'd known passion a time or two. But this was something far different. This was need. Raw. Urgent. Catching her by the throat and holding on until she couldn't breathe.

She felt his hands in her hair and something deep inside began twisting. Aching.

He pressed her back against the open door and kissed her long and slow and deep until they were both gasping. And still he kept his mouth on hers until the ache became a hungry yearning.

"Well, look at this, Octavia." Odelia Vandevere's wispy voice broke the spell. "I believe it's our dear Prudence and Mr. Lassiter."

Pru jerked back with such force she nearly fell. If it weren't for Micah's hands at her shoulders, keeping her steady, she would have embarrassed herself even further by running like a rabbit. As it was, she felt her cheeks turn every shade of red.

"Well." Octavia Vandevere paused a few steps from them, looking from one to the other. "It seems our young friends have been out on the town."

"Just...dinner." Pru knew her voice sounded breathy, but she felt the need to explain.

"Dinner. The two of you. Oh, that's grand. Just grand." Octavia studied the frown on Micah's face. Her own smile widened. "Well, don't let us keep you two from whatever you had in mind. Good night, Prudence, dear. Good night, Micah."

"'Night." Pru watched their retreating backs, then glanced shyly at Micah. "Good night."

"Yes. Good night." His frown was more pronounced as he turned away.

He waited until her door closed and the lock was thrown. Then he stepped into his own apartment.

He ought to be grateful for the arrival of those

two old busybodies. The way he'd been feeling with Pru in his arms, there was no telling where that kiss might have ended.

Not a good thing, he reminded himself for the hundredth time. He was quickly losing all objectivity where Prudence Street was concerned. And that could be deadly. For both of them.

Still, a part of him couldn't help wishing they'd had a minute more. The abruptness of their parting left him feeling a wave of bitter frustration.

That kiss had only whetted his appetite for more. Much more.

It would be, he realized, a long and frustrating night.

Chapter 6

"Why, Odelia." Octavia Vandevere beckoned to her sister. "Look who's out here in the garden. It's our dear Prudence."

Pru looked up from the bed of pansies she was weeding. "Good evening, Octavia. Odelia. You know I'm always out here on Saturday evenings, unless it's raining."

"Of course. A creature of habit, that's you, dear. I guess we just forgot." Octavia planted herself on a lovely stone bench and patted the spot beside her.

When Odelia joined her, they looked like two hungry cats about to pounce on an unsuspecting canary.

"So." Octavia glanced at her sister. "You and Micah Lassiter were out on a date last night."

"Not a date, exactly. He just took me to dinner."

"In my day, that was considered a date." Odelia's eyes were twinkling with mischief. "Where did you go?"

"To the Café Paris."

"Oh." Octavia clapped her hands together. "Sister and I love that place. It's so romantic. Did you sit indoors or out in the courtyard?"

Pru dug her hand trowel deep in the soil and removed several weeds, which she dropped into a bucket. "The courtyard. It was such a pretty night."

"That it was. I don't believe I heard your car." Odelia pulled a lace handkerchief from her pocket and touched it lightly to her forehead.

"We walked." Pru poked at another weed, trying to loosen the soil around it without disturbing the pretty violet pansy beside it.

"My," Odelia made a great show of folding the handkerchief precisely as it had been before returning it to her pocket. "It was the perfect night for walking. A full moon."

"Really?" Pru sat back on her heels and stripped off her gloves before turning toward the two old women. "I didn't notice."

"How could you miss it?" Octavia leaned forward and put a hand on Pru's arm. "Sister and I think Micah Lassiter is just about the best-looking young man we've seen in many a year. Isn't that right, Odelia?"

"Oh, indeed." Odelia lowered her voice as though sharing a great secret. "There's something so rugged and manly about him. With just the most fascinating hint of danger. He could certainly play the part of a hero in one of those adventure movies Sister and I love so much. Don't you agree, Prudence, dear?"

Before Prudence could say a word, the object of their discussion stepped into the garden and headed toward them. The two old women gave matching sighs.

"Good evening, ladies." Micah tucked his hands into the back pockets of his jeans. His first glimpse of Pru was, as always, a jolt to the system.

She was wearing simple cotton garden pants, the knees smudged from kneeling in the dirt. Her shirt was pale pink, with little embroidered flowers on the pocket. Her hair was tied back with a matching pink bandanna. There was a smudge of dirt on her left cheek, another on the tip of her nose. It was so endearing, it was all he could do to keep from touching a finger to the spot. "I hope I'm not interrupting anything."

"Not a thing, Micah." Octavia gave him a bright smile. "Doesn't our dear Prudence look just as pretty as her flowers?"

He nodded. "Even prettier, in fact."

At his scrutiny, Pru flushed.

"She has such a way with plants." Odelia gave a sigh. "Why, you wouldn't believe the way these gardens looked before she moved in here. Just a few bare patches of earth, and the professor's pitiful attempt at growing azaleas. And now look around you. Isn't this simply splendid?"

"Yes, it is." Micah glanced at his watch. "If you ladies will excuse me, I'm running up to the car wash."

Octavia stopped him with a hand on his. "Did you come out here for a reason, Micah?"

"No reason in particular." He shot a quick look at Pru. "I just wanted to say good evening. Now I'll say goodbye."

As he turned away, the two sisters hurried after him. When they caught up with him, Odelia quietly asked, "Do you think you'll be back before supper time?"

Micah considered. "I'm sure I will. Why? Is there something you need?"

"No, indeed. But it seems a shame not to take the time to enjoy such a beautiful spot on this perfect evening. Don't you think it might be fun to surprise our dear Prudence with a picnic?''

"A picnic." He seemed to mull that over a moment before giving a nod of his head. "Sounds like a great idea. Will you ladies join us?"

"Oh, aren't you sweet." The very thought generated such heat, Odelia began to fan herself.

Seeing it, Octavia gave her a quick nudge with her elbow. "That's very kind of you, Micah. But Sister and I have plans."

"We do?" Odelia turned big eyes on her older sister.

Octavia shot her a frown before saying, "You remember. Those plans we made for this evening."

"Oh. Oh, yes. Those—plans." She turned to Micah. "But I'm sure you and Prudence could have a grand picnic here alone in the garden."

Micah managed to hold back his laughter until he was in his car. Then, as he backed out of the garage and headed toward the car wash, he threw back his head and roared with laughter.

Those two old busybodies were about as subtle as a train wreck. And he'd lay odds they were having the time of their lives playing the oldest game in the book.

Not that he minded. It gave him the perfect excuse to be with Pru. Strictly for professional reasons, he told himself. He certainly couldn't protect her if he wasn't by her side. He'd spent the better part of the day watching her through the window. After all, that's what he was being paid to do. Just the sight of her working in the garden had brightened his day considerably.

There were certain perks to this job that made it all worthwhile.

"What's all this?" Pru looked up when Micah stepped into the garden, his arms laden with bags and cartons.

"Dinner." He set down his burden on the round, glass-topped table positioned beneath a rose arbor.

Pru walked toward him, stripping off her gloves. "Perfect timing. I forgot to eat today, and I'm positively starving. I hope you brought me a jumbo burger and fries."

"I brought something even better." He began setting out an assortment of fresh fruits and cheeses arranged on a covered crystal server, along with a basket of croissants. He removed the top from a silver bucket to reveal champagne on ice. A domed pedestal cake plate held tiny éclairs and hand-dipped chocolates.

He handed her a scented, moistened towel. She wiped her hands, then shook her head in amazement. "This doesn't look like something you ordered in a fast-food drive-through."

"You haven't heard of Instant Drive-Through Feast? It's the latest thing here in Georgetown."

She was laughing as she settled herself on the wrought-iron chair he was holding.

He popped the cork and filled two fluted glasses with champagne before handing one to her.

She sipped, then sat back with a sigh. "Oh, Micah. This is such a wonderful surprise."

"I'm glad you approve." He offered her a small crystal plate. "Fruit? Cheese?"

"Yes. To both." After her first bite she glanced over at him. "This tastes even better than it looks. Where in the world did you find all this?"

"There's a lovely little specialty shop nearby. I told them what I wanted, and by the time I returned from the car wash, they had everything ready. I didn't bother to ask how they did it. Maybe they have a magic genie in the back room."

She took another sip of champagne, and felt it go straight to her head. Or was it her heart? At this moment, she wasn't sure of anything except that no one had ever made her feel so special. So pampered. If there was a magic genie, she was certain it must be Micah Lassiter.

"How did you ever think of such a thing?"

"The idea was passed along to me by two very adorable angels."

Her hand paused in midair. "Angels?"

He nodded. "Named Octavia and Odelia."

"The Vandevere sisters dreamed this up?"

He chuckled. "Apparently they feel you and I are lacking a certain amount of romance in our lives. And they see it as their mission in life to change the situation." He picked up his glass and touched it to hers. "So here's to Octavia and Odelia Vandevere. I, for one, am grateful. If not for them, I'd probably be out in the garage polishing my car. Or up in my room going over financial statements for my company."

Pru laughed. "And I'd still be pulling weeds, and thinking about making a grilled-cheese sandwich to stave off hunger."

He lifted the cover from the fruit and cheese and waited for her to make another choice, before doing the same. After one taste he added, "This is definitely better than grilled cheese."

Pru gave a dreamy smile. "Much better."

The exotic food was enhanced by the serenity of the garden. Birds splashed in a fountain set in the middle of spectacular azaleas, in shades of pink and purple and white.

Micah sipped his champagne and sat back, taking the time to enjoy the view. He indicated the neat row of jewel-toned pansies edging a bed of white geraniums. "Where'd you learn to do all this?"

Pru's cheeks turned the most becoming shade of pink. "My father had a gardener who was always very patient with me. I think I must have asked him a million questions while I was growing up. And he never got cross with me, or suggested I go play somewhere. In fact, the hand trowel I use is one he gave me years ago so I could work alongside him."

"He was probably flattered that you took an interest in his work."

She nodded. "I suppose. But I think, too, he recognized a lonely little girl who was more comfortable with adults than with children."

There was something so wistful in her tone, Micah found himself taking her hand in his before he even realized what he was doing. "Who else did you pester while you were growing up?"

Pru absorbed the rush of heat, then felt her heart do a series of somersaults when he continued holding her hand. "The housekeeper. The cleaning staff. Our handyman. When I followed him up on the roof to see how he adjusted our satellite dish, he made me swear I'd never tell my father, or he'd have been fired on the spot."

Micah threw back his head and roared. "Smart man. What in the world were you doing on the roof?"

"I've always loved everything electronic. And I

just had to know about the satellite dish. How did it trap signals from so many locations? What would happen if it were moved slightly? Would it pick up more signals, or less? And why did storms over the Northwest blank out certain signals?''

He released her fingers and picked up his fluted glass. He needed a taste of champagne to cool his suddenly dry throat. It was amazing what the touch of her did to him. "Did you learn the answers?''

She nodded. "Of course. Then I drove him crazy until he taught me how to implant microchips in the coffeemaker and the dishwasher so I could program them from my laptop.''

Micah couldn't help grinning at the image of this very prim-and-proper young lady making the handyman's life miserable with impossible requests. "Did you have many chances to use this amazing skill?''

"Oh, yes. It drove my father crazy to find the coffee perking before anyone stepped into the kitchen.'' She rested her chin on her hands and regarded him. "Of course, it didn't take him long to figure out what I'd done.''

"Was he pleased or annoyed?''

"He pretended to be annoyed. But I've always thought he was secretly pleased. Did I mention that I was only nine at the time?'' She saw the look on Micah's face. "Sorry. I don't often admit to that.''

He was shaking his head, as though he couldn't quite believe what he'd just heard. "It had to be a little scary having a daughter that clever."

"Actually my father had no way of comparing me with other kids. So he just accepted that I was simply imitating him."

Micah's laughter grew. "I'll bet that made him glad he wasn't a bank robber."

"I never thought of that." She joined in the laughter. "Oh, look." She pointed to a tiny yellow-and-black bird darting among the flowers. "A goldfinch. I haven't seen one here before. Isn't it pretty?"

He looked over. "Like a canary, only bigger. Was bird watching another thing you pestered the gardener about?"

"Yes. In fact, I used to keep a journal of all the species that visited our garden each year."

He turned back, his eyes steady on hers. "The Vandevere sisters were right. You do know just about everything."

"If only that were true." She ducked her head, uncomfortable under his scrutiny. "What was your favorite subject in school?"

"Recess."

She couldn't help giggling. "And after that?"

"Math. Science."

"Really?" Now she was hooked. "Why did you like those best?"

"Math follows simple logic that never changes. I've always liked that."

Yes, she thought. A man like Micah Lassiter would prefer simple, straightforward logic. It suited him perfectly.

"As for science, there were all those unknowns." He chuckled. "I never could resist a challenge."

She leaned forward, her eyes shining. "I love mental challenges."

"How about physical ones?"

She shook her head. "I've always been too timid to accept physical challenges. I'm a good swimmer, but it never would have occurred to me to join the swim team in high school. The same for the equestrian team. I loved riding, and had my own mare when I was younger, but I just couldn't bear the thought of competing."

"There's nothing wrong with that. At least you got away from your laptop once in a—" His words trailed off as he stared beyond her.

She started to turn. "What is it?"

"Wait." He closed a hand over hers. "Don't turn just yet. Instead, let me help you to your feet."

He was already around the table and taking her hand in his, drawing her up and into his arms.

Her eyes narrowed. "What's going on, Micah?"

"It's the Vandevere sisters." He pressed his lips to a tangle of hair at her temple. "They're up on their rooftop garden watching us. I just caught sight of them hovering near the wall." He turned her slightly so she could take a peek without being too obvious. "And though I can't be certain, I think one of them is holding a pair of binoculars. At least that's what I think is glinting in Octavia's hands. See?"

Pru started to pull back. "Micah. They'll think we're kissing."

"Exactly." Without warning he drew her closer. His lips claimed hers. And though he'd intended it to be a joke on two old ladies, the joke was on him. Without any warning, he felt the quick sizzle of heat, and then the flood of warmth through his veins.

She tasted so sweet. Like her flowers. She felt so good here in his arms. So normal. As though he'd come home. And though he knew better, he couldn't bring himself to let go.

"Micah." She whispered the word against his lips, which only seemed to inflame him more.

"I know. We'll stop. In a minute." Right now, right this moment, it didn't matter that he had no right to touch her. All the blood seemed to have drained from his brain, emptying his mind, stealing his will.

Pru melted against him. She'd never felt arms this strong. Or a need so urgent. With just a single kiss he had the ability to wipe her mind clean. To eliminate all her inhibitions. It didn't matter that the Vandevere sisters were watching. Let the whole world watch. If she could, she would go on like this forever. Held in Micah's arms. Pressed to that hard, muscled body, while her bones melted, and her pulse rate speeded up until she felt as though she'd been running up a steep hill.

"Well." When at last he found the strength to lift his head, Micah continued holding her while he struggled for breath. "I guess I'd better start cleaning up."

"I'll…help you."

As they stepped apart and began clearing away the remains of their picnic, Pru shot him several quick glances.

What was it about this man that had her behaving so strangely? She had never in her life been so bold. And yet, if he were to kiss her again right this minute, she would react in exactly the same manner.

To end the awkward silence between them, she asked, "Is our audience still there?"

At her question, she saw Micah glance toward

the rooftop garden. Then he smiled, and she felt the quick flutter around her heart.

"Still there. And now I think I detect two pairs of binoculars. I wonder what they'll do when we leave?"

"Maybe it's time to find out."

They were grinning like two conspirators as they carried the bags indoors. But once inside, they went their separate ways, Pru to her apartment to clean up, and Micah to try to get some work done.

As they parted, Micah stood in the doorway and waited until Pru's door closed. The last thing he saw was her smile as she turned away. He waited until she threw the lock before closing the door to the professor's apartment.

It was time for a little soul-searching, he realized. Things were going in a direction he hadn't anticipated.

He needed to back off and give her, and himself, some space before this got out of hand.

Chapter 7

"Allen Street here."

"Allen." Micah sat at Professor Loring's desk, glancing at the stack of reports he was preparing to fax. "Will just told me there was another contact. Did it contain a threat?"

"Not a threat, exactly. Just more rambling and twisted anger. But my people believe he's slipping closer to the edge." Street's voice sounded rough with nerves. "I found the e-mail this morning when I got to the office. The FBI is already analyzing it."

"Do your operatives think they're getting any closer to learning this guy's identity?"

"They say it's only a matter of time."

Time. Micah tried to keep the edge of annoyance from his tone. "Allen, I've been on the job for more than two weeks now. Two weeks of spending every waking hour with your daughter, on one pretext or another. But the lies are stretching thin. I've already had the Children's Village beef up their security as much as possible. They've cooperated completely. I can't spend too many more days there without drawing suspicion." He paused, then decided to charge full-speed ahead. "I think it's time you told Pru the truth."

"You've had time to get to know my daughter, Micah. I'm sure you've noticed that our relationship is...strained, to say the least. The more I try to reel her in, the more she'll just push away."

"Do you think it's fair to put her in harm's way without any warning?"

"Harm's way?" Street's tone sharpened. "That's why you're there. To see that she isn't harmed."

"But I have to keep lying about who I am and what I'm doing here, and I'm tired of the lies."

"I see."

Micah heard the edge of anger.

"So this isn't about Pru. It's about you."

Maybe it was, Micah thought wearily. He and Pru had been seeing each other daily at the Children's Village, as well as every evening. The truth was, he'd begun to look forward to their time together. After work they'd explored half a dozen different restaurants, as well as every carryout in the area. They'd been careful not to let themselves get caught up in any romantic knots since the picnic, but they both seemed to sense that a storm was building. A simple touch was enough to trigger lightning and thunder. What would they do if things slipped out of control?

"I don't like lying, Allen."

"I'm not worried about offending your particular code of ethics, Lassiter. All that matters to me is my daughter's happiness. And since my people don't feel that there's been any threat to her personal safety yet, I'm going to have to refuse your request. I want Pru kept in the dark about this."

"It's your show, Allen."

"That's right. I'm the producer, director, and until this nut is caught, the reluctant star. And I pray every day that it's all a false alarm." The voice at the other end of the line sounded suddenly exhausted beyond belief. The tension was beginning to take its toll on everyone. "Fax those reports now. I'll have Will contact you as soon as there are any leads in this case."

"Right." Micah hung up the phone, then began faxing the documents.

He glanced out the window and caught sight of Prudence walking along the flagstone path in the garden with Randall and Helena Crispin. As he studied her, Micah found himself frowning.

He'd expected the daughter of one of the richest men in the country to be a pampered ice princess. A queen of excess. Instead, he'd found her to be as normal as the girl next door. A bright, funny, shy, sweet and very vulnerable woman.

And he was falling for her. Falling hard.

The last thing he'd expected was to lose his heart to the woman he'd been hired to protect. But that's what was happening here. And he couldn't afford to have feelings for her. It went against everything he'd ever learned. He needed to keep a distance between himself and the client, for the sake of objectivity.

The client.

Every day that passed made it harder for him to think of Prudence Street as a client. Still, if he wanted to keep her safe from all harm, that's exactly what he needed to do.

He put in a call to his office, then sat tapping a pencil as he waited for the phone to be answered. He knew his business was being carefully managed in his absence. But with every passing day he found himself wishing he'd refused Allen Street's initial request.

If he'd never met Prudence Street, he could have spared himself a lot of misery.

Pru stirred the spaghetti sauce, tasted, then turned the heat down to simmer. Instead of eating in the kitchen, she'd decided to set two places on the glass-topped table in the great room, to take advantage of the garden view.

When she'd finally summoned the courage to ask Micah to dinner, he'd made it so easy. But then, Micah Lassiter seemed to make everything easy. Since he'd taken over the professor's apartment, her whole life felt as though it had changed. From winter to spring. From barren to blooming. And she had changed with it. From shy to bold. Well, she amended as she fussed with the candles in crystal holders, not yet bold. But not quite as shy as before.

At the knock on the door, she hurried to peek out before throwing the safety.

"Hello. You're right on time."

"When a man's hungry, he's never late." Micah stood on the threshold with both hands behind his back. "Which do you choose? Door number one or door number two?"

This was a playful side to the man that never failed to surprise her. She seemed as delighted as a child at the game. With a laugh she touched a hand to his left arm. "This one."

"Good choice. That's door number one." He brought his hand around with a flourish to reveal a glorious bouquet of spring flowers. A mass of deep purple lilacs and golden daffodils, delicate white baby's breath and trailing ivy.

"Oh, Micah." Pru buried her face in the bouquet and breathed deeply. "They're beautiful."

"Almost as beautiful as the woman holding them." He winked. "Now, how about door number two?"

"More surprises?" She waited while he brought his right hand from behind him to reveal a bottle of red wine. Seeing it she laughed. "You're going to spoil me."

He tugged on a lock of her hair. "You? Not a chance. But I think it would be fun to try."

"Come on. The wine will be perfect with my pasta." She led the way to the kitchen. After handing him a corkscrew, she filled an elegant crystal vase with water and carefully arranged the flowers before carrying them to the other room, where she placed them on the mantel. Their perfume quickly filled the room.

When she returned to the kitchen, Micah was just pouring wine into two stem glasses. He handed one to her.

She accepted it, feeling the quick flutter of nerves when their fingers brushed. "What are we drinking to?"

He touched his glass to hers. "To good friends."

She struggled to keep her smile in place. She'd foolishly hoped he would say something more romantic. And all because of Octavia and Odelia. Those two old sweethearts were constantly putting thoughts in her head. Making her think about things better left alone.

"To good friends," she said as she lifted the glass to her lips.

"And, judging by the wonderful aroma in this kitchen, good food as well." He glanced toward the stove. "Is that spaghetti sauce I smell?"

"I hope you like pasta."

"I love it." He turned toward the loaf of garlic bread. "Want me to slice this?"

"If you'd like. I was just going to fix our salads." She tore lettuce, chopped fresh green tomatoes, peppers and chives from the farmers' market, and tossed them with a little olive oil and balsamic vinegar.

While she worked she could feel him nearby, slicing the bread and arranging it on a platter. It should have seemed awkward having Micah working beside her in the kitchen, but instead it felt comfortable. There was something about this quiet, competent man that put her at ease. That is, until he touched her. Then sparks flew, setting off all manner of fires inside her.

Micah picked up the platter. "Where would you like this?"

She nearly jumped before she managed to take a quiet breath. "I thought we'd eat in the great room."

"Okay. I'll be right back."

When he left, she sipped her wine to soothe her dry throat. Then she tossed angel-hair pasta into boiling water.

By the time Micah returned to the kitchen, she was draining the pasta. He leaned a hip against the counter and watched. "I'd say you've done this a time or two."

She laughed. "Pasta's easy. It's one of the first things I learned to make for myself when I left home." She arranged it on a platter, then added the sauce.

Micah moved up beside her. "Want me to carry this?"

"All right. I'll bring the wine." She followed him to the table and topped off their glasses, before lighting the candles.

He held her chair, then sat across from her. He nodded toward the garden outside her window. "Great view."

"That's why I wanted to eat in here. I love looking at the flowers."

"According to the Vandevere sisters, you've worked miracles out there."

Pru laughed. "You know how Octavia and Odelia carry on. The truth is, Professor Loring was doing a fine job on the garden. But the poor dear just didn't have enough time to spend."

"And you did?"

She ducked her head. "My social calendar wasn't overcrowded."

"By design, I'd say." He broke off a piece of garlic bread. "How did you happen to choose this apartment building? It's not exactly geared to the hip party crowd."

"A friend of the family recommended it. When I investigated it, I found it to my liking."

"And all these exciting neighbors?"

Her flush deepened. "I've always been more comfortable around older people."

"I see." He sat back. "I didn't realize I was over the hill."

"I didn't mean you..." She stopped when she saw his quick, devastating smile and realized he was teasing her. She decided to relax and play along. "Well, I have been meaning to ask how old you are."

"Thirty-three. Practically ready for social security. How about you?"

"Twenty-seven. I'll be twenty-eight next month."

Though he'd known that, it was a jolt to hear her say it aloud. She seemed, in some ways, so childlike. There was a freshness, an innocence about her that belied her age. As though she'd sprung, fully grown, without any of life's normal experiences.

He filled his plate with pasta, then nodded toward hers. "Did you want some of this? Or are you waiting to see if I survive before you taste it?"

She was laughing as she held out her plate. "You're lucky I'm willing to share. Usually I eat this much all by myself."

He shot her an admiring glance. "Sorry. There's no way that little body could hold all this."

"Don't be fooled. I may forget to eat, but when I make my special spaghetti sauce, I'm like a bottomless pit."

He tasted, then gave a look of surprise. "This is even better than Pop's." He lowered his voice. "Of course, we can't let him know that. It would break his heart."

"Your grandfather's a good cook?"

"Yeah, he exchanges recipes with every woman in the neighborhood. When we were younger, he used to take us to the playground and sit there with all the women, gabbing about housework and yellow waxy buildup on his kitchen floors. The old schemer plied them all with his charm. My mother used to accuse him of having more lady friends than she had."

"He sounds delightful."

Micah sat back, sipping his wine. "Yeah. He's pretty amazing. The day my dad died, he stepped in and kept my family going. And he's been there ever since."

Pru twisted the napkin in her lap, thinking about how different their families were. She loved hearing stories about Micah's grandfather and mother, his sister and brothers. It would be fun to talk about her own father in that same light manner. But though she wanted to tell him about her background, she held back, afraid it would change the easy relationship she and Micah had begun to develop.

In the past, men had always treated her differently the minute they learned that she was the daughter of Allen Street. Either they were intimidated by his enormous wealth, and backed off completely, or else they tried to force a relationship, not because of her, but rather because of what they stood to gain.

It always came down to the money.

With Micah, it was different. He had no idea who she was. He liked her just for herself. This friendship was too new, too fragile, to risk damaging with the truth. And so she resisted the urge to take him into her confidence.

"More pasta?" His voice was low and easy, as though not wanting to intrude on her thoughts.

She looked up and saw him studying her. If she didn't know better, she'd think he could even read her mind. "No, thanks. I think I'd better quit while I can still walk. Besides, I have dessert."

"Why didn't you say so?" He twirled the last of his spaghetti on his fork and sat back with a smile. "Can I help?"

"No. I can manage." She pushed away from the table. "I'll be right back."

When she was gone, Micah's eyes narrowed in thought. Pru never talked about her family, except in generalizations. It would make things easier if she did. But for now, he would have to play along and pretend to be ignorant of her background.

Even though he'd given his word to Allen Street, he hated the lies.

"Here we are." She set a plate down in front of him and watched his reaction to the brownie, smothered in ice cream and fudge sauce.

He looked over as she sat across from him. "This is like poison to the arteries. If I eat this,

I'll have to do a hundred push-ups to work it off. You're trying to kill me, aren't you?''

She couldn't help laughing. "I'm going to enjoy this with absolutely no guilt."

"Fine. As for me, I'm going to have just one taste." He took a bite and closed his eyes. Then, with a roguish grin, he cleaned his plate before sitting back with a sigh. "Two hundred push-ups. And I'll curse your name with every one of them."

A signal rang in the kitchen.

Pru started to get up. "That's the coffee."

"I'll get it. I need the exercise." He touched a hand to her shoulder and hurried away.

When he was gone, she sat very still, feeling the warmth of his touch. It had been so long since he'd touched her. That thought rankled.

She wanted him to. Wanted him to kiss her the way he had that day in the garden. But ever since then, he seemed to be holding her at a distance.

She'd thought at first it was her imagination. But as the days had gone on, she'd had to accept the fact that his withdrawal was deliberate.

"Here we are."

As he returned with the coffee, Pru took several deep breaths and forced herself to relax. After all, the evening wasn't over yet. And she intended to do everything in her power to get him to kiss her before he left. Even if it meant throwing herself at him like some sort of silly, love-struck teen.

Chapter 8

As she sipped her coffee, Pru studied Micah by the light of the flickering candles. He was such a contradiction. She couldn't figure him out. He had that wonderful Irish humor that could make her laugh no matter what her mood. And yet she sensed a darkness in him as well. A private, mysterious place inside him where she was never allowed to go.

He seemed absolutely fearless. Almost reckless. He reminded her of a magnificent wild creature. One that would survive the most impossible odds. And yet, on those rare occasions when he'd let down his guard, she thought she'd detected pain.

A wound, perhaps to his heart. It was her nature to want to soothe, to help in some way, but she didn't know how. She hated this timid streak in her that kept her from reaching out. Though she'd made great strides, she knew she still had a long way to go.

Micah glanced over. "You're quiet tonight."

Her head came up. "Am I?"

He finished his coffee and glanced at the clock. "I should go."

"Not yet." Pru's protest was a little too sharp. When he looked at her she flushed and added in a softer tone, "The garden is so pretty this time of night. And we both need to walk off those calories. Walk with me, Micah."

"All right. Good idea."

She led the way to the French doors and unlocked them before stepping out into the warm spring air. Micah trailed behind, his narrowed gaze sweeping the shadows before falling into step beside her.

She paused. "Why do you do that?"

"Do what?"

"Look around so carefully before taking a step."

"It goes with the territory, I guess." He reminded himself that he'd have to be more careful. Pru was a lot more observant than he'd realized.

"I suppose security people are much like police detectives. They see the seamy side of life that the rest of us aren't exposed to." She glanced over. "Doesn't that make it harder to enjoy your life?"

"Not necessarily. It certainly makes us more cautious. But maybe, after seeing how fragile life can be, it also makes us more eager to reach out and grab what pleasure we can from this life before it's snatched away."

"Is that your motto?" She paused to brush her hand over the ornamental scrollwork on a garden sculpture. "Seize the moment?"

"Not exactly. I guess it's more like seize the criminal before he seizes me." The look on her face had him chuckling. "Just teasing."

He lifted a finger to her cheek before he'd had time to think. Bad idea, he realized. Touching her always affected him.

Before he could do any more damage, he deliberately lowered his hand to his side, where he clenched it into a fist. "Then, when my job's finished, I'll think about seizing whatever pleasure is left."

"So, the job always comes first?"

"That's right."

Pru paused beside a fountain where water spilled from a small basin into a larger one. Micah studied the way she looked in profile, with moonlight in her hair. Like an angel that had just dropped down from heaven. There was such sweetness in her. She was, without a doubt, one of life's gentle creatures. Right now, watching her, he had to agree with her father's decision. Pru deserved the freedom to pursue whatever lifestyle she wanted, without the added burden of fear.

"What frightens you the most, Pru?"

She seemed startled by the question. After a moment of silence, she said, "Storms."

"Storms?"

She nodded. "Thunder and lightning. One of my earliest memories is climbing up on my mother's lap and crying during a storm. I felt safe with her. Secure. Then, after she was...gone, our housekeeper found me huddled in her closet during a storm, wrapped in one of her dresses. I remember being carried kicking and screaming to my father, who couldn't understand why I could be afraid of a simple summer storm. But shortly after that he decided to hire a tutor and keep me out of school. After that, my world seemed to shrink more and more until all it consisted of was my father and my home, and our small circle of friends."

"How old were you when your mother died?"

"Three."

"And your father never married again?"

She shook her head. "He said his job and his daughter were all he needed."

"And now?"

She shrugged, clearly uncomfortable. "I hated leaving him, knowing he'd be all alone. But I had to get away or be suffocated."

They walked in silence for several minutes. It occurred to Micah that this was the most she'd ever told him about herself. Though he'd known about her mother's untimely death, he never would have guessed her fear of storms.

Pru glanced over. "Margot Jamison seemed quite impressed with the improvements you've made in security at the Children's Village."

"I just tightened things a bit."

"She said you did everything free of charge."

"It wouldn't be right to charge a charity."

"They have a budget for such things."

He shrugged. "I feel better knowing they'll use the money for something else. Besides, I took a lot of liberties, adding things just to satisfy my own sense of security."

"Isn't it a coincidence that Margot happened to call you so soon after you moved in next to me?"

"Yeah." He paused along the path to study a section of the garden devoted to roses. "These are really beautiful. What're they called?"

She touched a hand to the bright red blossoms.

"Daredevils. A hybrid climber that's ever blooming. They make a spectacular display."

"And this?" He cupped a tall bloom and breathed in the perfume.

"Night Magic." It occurred to Pru that he had once again cleverly manipulated the conversation away from himself. Not that she minded. She never tired of talking about the flowers in her garden. Still, it had been an almost seamless move on his part. As though he'd had plenty of experience changing directions whenever anyone got too close.

"It smells like you." In the stillness of the night his voice seemed even deeper, sending shivers along her spine.

"Thank you." She stopped beside him. "I'll take that as a compliment."

"That's how it was meant." When he straightened, their shoulders brushed.

She smiled before taking his arm. "Over here I've planted a border of bocovia. As it grows it will spill over the stone retaining wall in a cascade of white starflowers and deep green ivy. It makes a really spectacular display."

He wasn't really listening to what she was saying. It was, he realized, just enough to hear that soft, throaty voice whispering over his senses. To have her arm linked with his, their shoulders and hips brushing as they walked. It was the sweetest torture of his life to be this close, to be nearly overcome with the need to taste, to touch, to take, and to know that he was duty-bound to resist.

"I was thinking of adding a bed of begonias here. They have the loveliest jewel-tone blossoms that seem to just shimmer in sunlight." She looked up expectantly. "What do you think?"

For the space of a heartbeat he didn't say a word as he stared at her mouth, curved into the most appealing smile.

"Micah?" Her smile deepened and she touched a finger to the frown line between his eyebrows. "Where are you?"

"Somewhere I shouldn't be." His tone was curt. "I think it's time we went inside."

"All right." Pru moved along beside him, matching his impatient strides.

Her heart was racing, and her throat had gone dry. He'd wanted to kiss her. But something had stopped him.

Was she sending mixed signals? Did he somehow think she didn't want him? If so, she intended to set him straight. Starting tonight.

As they opened the French doors and stepped into her apartment, she glanced at the clock on the mantel and caught sight of his bouquet. "I loved the flowers, Micah. And the walk in the garden."

"I'm glad. Though they were little enough payment for dinner." He started toward the foyer, with Pru trailing behind.

At the door he paused to give her a smile. "Thanks, Pru. It's been a great evening."

She deliberately planted herself in front of the door. Though her heart was pounding, she was determined to stand her ground. No more timid mouse for her. It was time to go after what she wanted. She touched a hand to his. "It doesn't have to end yet, Micah."

He couldn't have been more stunned if she'd stripped naked. He could feel himself sweating. "I wish I could stay but..."

"You strike me as a man who does exactly as he pleases." She ran her fingers up his arm as she inched closer, until their bodies were brushing.

He closed his eyes a moment as feelings rocketed through him. How the hell was he supposed to gracefully extract himself from this?

What a mess. The very thing he wanted most was the thing he couldn't have. Not if he hoped to do the job he'd been hired to do.

Though it would be forced, he decided to try for humor. "Are you trying to seduce me, Pru?"

"And what if I am?"

"You don't know anything about me. For all you know, I could be a mass murderer who likes to take his victims to bed before carving them into little pieces.''

Instead of backing off, she laughed as she curled her arms around his neck and pressed herself against him. ''I can see that you've been working in security too long, Micah Lassiter. You're starting to sound like one of those television tabloid teasers during ratings sweeps season.''

''All right.'' When had the shrinking violet become this bold femme fatale? However it had happened, she was having the desired effect on him. He was fully aroused. And if he didn't get out of here quickly, there was no telling how the evening would end.

He reached up and slowly, deliberately, removed her arms from around his neck. Then, before she could reach for him again, he caught her roughly by the shoulders and held her a little away.

''Sex isn't a game I take lightly.'' His eyes were hot and fierce.

''And you think I do?'' For a moment she felt a wave of humiliation and lowered her head, refusing to meet his look. Then, as embarrassment gave way to anger, she shook off his touch and took a step back, tossing her head. ''If you knew anything about me, Micah Lassiter, you'd know that I don't rush into things without thinking them through. I thought…'' She blinked, afraid for a moment her temper was so great she might embarrass herself by crying. "I thought I knew you. I thought you wanted what I wanted."

"You don't know me, Pru." His voice was rough with passion. "You only think you do. You think because I enjoy pasta and walks in the garden, that I'll be this perfect gentleman who returns your kisses with a few chaste kisses of my own. Maybe you've imagined that we'll even have a nice tumble in bed, and then I'll go my merry way and you'll go yours." His tone lowered. "If you knew what I really wanted, you'd be so shocked you'd order me out of your apartment and never let me inside again."

She squared her shoulders. "I don't believe you. You're just trying to frighten me."

"Am I?" Without thinking, his hand snaked out, closing around her wrist.

She jerked back but he snagged her other wrist, imprisoning her without even a struggle. Keeping his eyes steady on hers, he dragged her into his arms and crushed her mouth beneath his. Heat poured between them. A raging inferno that had them diving fully into the kiss and taking all they could.

They were both gasping for air when he finally lifted his head. But instead of releasing her, he kissed her again with such passion, he drove her back against the wall, pinning her there with his body. And all the while his mouth savaged hers, and his free hand moved over her, touching her at will.

She was so soft. So small. So perfect. And he wanted, with every fiber of his being, to take her here and now.

"Micah." At her little cry he lifted his head and released her wrists.

Then, feeling remorse, he touched a fingertip to her mouth. Just a touch, but it was enough to have him murmuring an apology as he brushed his lips ever so lightly over hers.

"I'm sorry, Pru. I wanted to…" The words ended in a growl as he took the kiss deeper.

All his good intentions fled as the kiss softened and seemed to go on and on, spinning entirely out of control. "I wanted to show you the real me. And to be honest, I wanted to frighten you."

"You did."

"And now?" His mind clouded over as his hands moved along her spine, igniting fires everywhere.

"Now I'm terrified." She made a low moaning sound in her throat and clutched at his waist, afraid that at any moment her knees would buckle and she would slip to the floor.

"Me, too." He had to get out of here. Had to.

Because if he didn't make good his escape right this minute, there would be no turning back.

He brought his hands to her upper arms and drew her away. For a minute he merely held her there while he dragged air into his starving lungs. He could see the way she was struggling for breath.

At last he found his voice. "I'm going now. We'll both have clearer heads in the morning."

"Is that what you think, Micah?"

He turned away, unable to bear the look in her eyes. "Lock your door, Pru. And engage your alarm."

He yanked open the door and pulled it shut behind him, then waited until he heard the click of the dead bolt.

As he entered Professor Loring's apartment, he glanced at the decanter of aged whiskey on a sideboard.

He wasn't much of a drinking man. But tonight he was about to make an exception.

Chapter 9

"Look at him." Margot Jamison stood by the window in Pru's tiny office and watched as Micah examined the newly installed cameras in the parking area. "As my thirteen-year-old daughter would say, talk about your major hunk."

"Really?" Pru was still reeling from that scene with Micah the night before, and determined not to dwell on it. "I hadn't noticed."

Margot laughed. "If that's true, you need an eye exam." She continued watching him. "I don't think I've ever met anyone as thorough as Micah Lassiter. Not that I'm surprised. Knowing his family, I'd expect nothing less."

Pru looked up from her computer monitor. "What about his family?"

Margot leaned a hip against the file cabinet. "Folks who live around here know all about them. His father was a decorated police officer when he was gunned down in the line of duty."

Pru carefully folded her hands in her lap. "He never mentioned it."

"I guess it's not something a man would talk about. Especially a man like Micah Lassiter." She glanced beyond Pru to her computer monitor. "You've got an e-mail."

Pru typed a prompt to open her mail. As soon as she began scanning it, she made a sound of surprise.

"What is it?" Margot moved closer, reading over Pru's shoulder.

The words seemed to leap out at her.

Now I've found you, little lamb. Prepare to be sacrificed for the sins of your father.

Pru shook her head. "This doesn't make any sense. It must be a prank."

When she made a move to delete the message, Margot clamped a hand over her wrist. "Wait a minute. Leave it alone. I want Micah to take a look at this."

"Micah? Why?"

"Because," Margot turned to the door, "in his line of work, he'd know whether it's a joke or a threat. I'll be right back."

When she was gone, Pru read the e-mail again. This time as she read each word she felt a tingling at the back of her neck. If the note was meant as a prank, it was having the desired effect. It was positively creepy.

Within minutes Margot was back with Micah.

He showed no emotion as he read the words on the screen. His tone was equally flat. "I want you to print out a copy of this, and then keep this post as new mail until I can have someone here to read and evaluate it."

Pru glanced at his face, wishing she could read it. But he gave nothing away. "You don't think it's a prank?"

"It could be. But there's no harm in checking it out." He glanced at his watch before pulling a cell phone from his pocket. "I'll have someone here within the hour."

He stepped quickly from her office and made his way down the hallway. When he'd put enough distance between himself and them, he dialed the private number of her father.

"Allen Street."

"Micah Lassiter here. Our guy's found your daughter's e-mail address."

The voice at the other end sharpened considerably. "How do you know?"

"She just received one of his e-mails. I've asked her to save it. Maybe the FBI can trace it."

"I'll have someone there immediately. Is she upset?"

"Not particularly. I didn't let on that it was much to worry about."

"Good." There was an audible sigh. "Is she at home or at work?"

"At work. Now are you going to let her in on what's happening?"

"No." Street's tone lowered with feeling. "It wouldn't have been too difficult for our guy to track her online screen name. It's one she's had for years. But that's a far cry from knowing where she is. For all he knows, she could be on another continent."

"Maybe. But that's an awfully big risk."

"Just stick close to her, Lassiter, until we get this guy."

"You can count on it." Micah disconnected, then decided to stay busy until he had a chance to speak with the FBI operatives.

He spotted them the minute they arrived. The man and woman were dressed in dark suits as they emerged from a van. They shook hands with him, spoke briefly, then followed him to Pru's office.

She looked up as they paused in the doorway.

"Prudence Street, this is Linda and Phil. I thought I'd buy you a coffee next door while they check out your computer."

"But they might need my help."

"Trust me. They're computer experts."

Pru glanced from Micah to the stone-faced couple, then nodded. "All right. If you say so."

He had a hand under her elbow and was steering her out the door before she had time to think.

Once they were next door, he led her to a table in the sunshine and signaled to the waitress. Within minutes, Mindy was at their table with her usual smile. "This is a surprise. I didn't see you two earlier today."

Micah returned the smile. "We were saving our appetite for good coffee until we had time to really appreciate it."

"I'll bring the usual." She looked from one to the other. "How about a sandwich to go with it?"

"Nothing for me," Pru said.

Micah shook his head. "Sorry. Just coffee."

When she was gone he sat back and watched as Pru kept glancing at her office across the street. She waited until their coffee had been delivered before speaking. "What did you make of that, Micah?"

He shrugged. "Hard to say. It could be somebody having fun with you."

"That wasn't funny. It was eerie."

"Yeah." He sipped his coffee, his eyes narrowed in thought. "It takes all kinds."

"Have you seen a lot of this in your business?"

"Some."

She twisted her hands together on the tabletop. "Are they always pranks? Or do some of them turn out to be...more?"

He put a hand over hers, wishing he could do more to comfort her. "Most are just harmless pranks. People who get a rush out of scaring others. Let Linda and Phil do their job. They're good at it. Whatever this turns out to be, they'll take care of it."

She nodded. When he lifted his hand from hers, she picked up her cup and drained it.

She gave him a weak smile. "It's lucky for me you were here today. I thought your work at the Children's Village was over."

"It is, for the most part. I just wanted to check out a few things." He looked up and saw the hand at the window of her office, a signal that the FBI had finished their work. "Let's get back now."

As she followed him across the street, Pru found

herself wondering again about the heat she felt whenever Micah touched her. A simple press of his hand on hers was all that was needed to light the torch. She had no doubt he felt it, too. But he seemed determined not to act on his feelings.

Maybe she ought to be grateful. There was so much about him she didn't know. But the fact Margot had revealed explained so much. No wonder he was tight-lipped about himself.

She pulled herself back from her troubling thoughts as she approached her office.

The young woman, Linda, offered her hand. "Thanks for allowing us access to your computer, Ms. Street. We've forwarded this message to the appropriate authorities, who have promised to look into it. If it's anything more than a prank, we'll deal with it."

"Will I get a report of some kind?"

Linda nodded. "If anything comes of it, you'll be notified."

"Thank you." Pru watched as the man and woman left her office carrying several file folders.

"Well." Micah tucked his hands into his back pockets. "Guess I'll check out the rest of the security equipment. I'll be back later."

Pru nodded and settled herself at her desk. A few minutes later, as she opened a file cabinet, she glanced out the window and saw Micah talking with the couple at their van.

It occurred to her that the three of them looked much more comfortable now that they were out of earshot. She couldn't shake the uneasy feeling that she was their topic of conversation.

"Hi." Micah stood in the doorway of Pru's office.

She glanced over with a look of surprise. "I thought you'd left hours ago. I haven't seen you around all afternoon."

"I did a tour of the complex and checked out all the equipment. Are you ready to leave?"

"I won't be going straight home." Pru opened a drawer and slung her purse over her shoulder. "I need a few things at the store."

"So do I." His smile was quick and easy. "Why don't I follow you?"

"All right." As Pru made her way from the office to her car, the uneasy feeling was back. The feeling that everything Micah did had a specific purpose. That he never did anything by accident.

Except those few times when he'd kissed her. She was certain those had been purely spontaneous.

She dug her keys out of her pocket and pressed

the unlock button. Before she could reach for the door, Micah was there, holding it open.

"Thanks." She settled herself inside and turned the ignition as Micah climbed into his own car beside hers.

By the time she was driving away, he was right on her tail. On a whim she decided to test her theory. At the end of the block, she slowed down as the light turned amber, then raced ahead, barely making it through before the light turned red. When she glanced in her rearview mirror, she saw Micah's car behind hers. And though she couldn't see his face through the tinted windows, she found herself laughing.

"Well, well, Mr. Lassiter. You do stay close, don't you?"

She turned into the parking lot of a small specialty store. As she stepped out of her car, Micah walked up behind her. And though his features were composed, she had the feeling that his temper was close to the surface.

"Do you usually run through red lights?"

She gave him a bright smile. "Only when I'm distracted. I shouldn't be too long. What are you hoping to buy?"

"This and that. How about you?"

She merely smiled as she stepped inside and began circling the aisles. Two could play the silent game.

An hour later she wheeled her cart toward her car and began unloading the half-dozen bags of goodies. Most of the groceries she'd purchased weren't even things she particularly liked or needed. But she'd had a grand time testing Micah's patience. His own cart was practically empty, but he'd managed to linger until she reached the checkout. Then he'd stepped up behind her.

After unloading his cart he helped her with hers, stowing bags in her small trunk.

"Thanks, Micah." Because she was feeling a little twinge of guilt, she called out, "This time I'll follow you."

He nodded and climbed into his car, leaving it to idle until he saw Pru turn the ignition of her car. As he started moving ahead, he saw her headlights behind him. He paused to allow traffic to pass, then started out of the parking lot. Just then a car speeded up and he was forced to brake suddenly. A second later he felt the impact as Pru's car plowed into the back of his.

He was glowering as he left his car idling and walked back to hers. He tore open her door. "Didn't you see my brake lights?"

"Yes." In the dim lights she looked unnaturally pale. "I tried to stop. But my brakes didn't work."

His anger was gone instantly. He could see her hands on the wheel. They were trembling.

When he finally spoke, his voice was dangerously soft. "Step out a minute, Pru, and come sit in my car."

He kept an arm around her shoulder as he helped her into the passenger side of his car. Then he returned to her car and backed it slowly away from his. When he touched the brakes, her little car continued backing up. When it rolled to a stop, he shifted gears and started it forward. Again, when he tried to brake, the car continued moving.

With a thoughtful look he drove it to the back of the parking lot and allowed it to roll to a gradual stop. Then he pulled out his cell phone and spoke into it. Minutes later he joined Pru in his car and drove it to a spot beside hers.

"What are we doing?"

"Waiting here for a tow truck."

She shivered. "I hate to think what would have happened to me if you hadn't stopped just then, Micah. If I hadn't discovered this until I was in the thick of traffic…"

"Hey." He touched a hand to her cheek, then just as quickly withdrew it. "It's just a little problem with the brakes. It'll be good as new in a day or two."

He glanced up as the tow truck arrived. "You stay here. I'll take care of this."

Pru watched as he spoke with the man in the truck. They conferred for several minutes before Micah returned to his car.

"The garage will phone me as soon as they have the problem fixed."

Shortly after they had pulled away, Pru sat up with a start. "My groceries. They're still in the trunk."

"Sorry. Want to go back for them?"

She shook her head. "The tow truck is probably miles from here by now. I guess I'll just forget about dinner tonight."

"Tell you what." His mind was sharp and clear as he began mulling over the various scenarios. This could have been a deliberate attempt to kill her. Messing with her brakes could be intended as a warning. It could be someone's idea of a cruel hoax. At any rate, if the sabotage was deliberate, it had to have occurred here in the parking lot. If her car had been tampered with at the Children's Village, it would have been caught on one of the security cameras. And that meant that the culprit could still be watching. And following.

There was, of course, a very slim chance that this had been an accident. Micah would have to wait until his operative got back to him with a report. His last words to his man had been that he wanted every inch of Prudence Street's vehicle checked until all facts were determined. There was no room for error. And no room for doubt.

"I know a great little spot. It's quite a drive from here, but well worth the time. Want to give it a try?"

Pru took a long, deep breath and forced herself to relax. After all, nobody had been hurt. It had been a simple enough accident. By tomorrow, she'd have forgotten all about it.

She nodded. "All right. Sounds like fun."

Fun. Beside her, Micah's easy smile faded as he watched every headlight trailing him. Somehow, the idea of having a leisurely dinner while some nutcase was out there plotting destruction was not his idea of fun.

Still, he was getting ahead of himself. He would have to patiently wait for the report before knowing whether this was deliberate or accidental. If his instincts were correct, this charade would be all over. Pru would go home to Seattle until the guy was caught.

Even though it was what he wanted, Micah found no satisfaction in the idea. The thought of never seeing Prudence Street again caused a hollow feeling in the pit of his stomach.

Mere hunger pangs, he told himself sternly. But the thought of food suddenly made him queasy.

Chapter 10

"Micah Lassiter." The owner of the rustic inn in the Virginia hills greeted them warmly. "It's been too long."

"Yes it has, Joe." Micah forced himself to relax. They'd been on the road for more than two hours. He'd changed directions so often, he was absolutely convinced that no one had followed them. "I'd like you to meet Prudence Street."

"Ms. Street." The owner glanced around. "How about a nice private booth?"

Micah nodded and took Pru's arm as they made their way across the room.

"I have a bottle of chardonnay I've been saving

for a special occasion.'' The owner signaled to a waitress. "Bring a bottle of my private stock and two glasses.''

Within minutes the bottle had been opened, their glasses filled and pleasantries exchanged before the waitress took their dinner order.

When they were finally alone, Micah glanced across the table at Prudence. "You okay?''

"I'm fine." She sipped her wine before glancing around. "I assume you come here often."

"I've known Joe since high school. This has always been my great escape.''

"From what?''

"Life.'' He shrugged. "If there are problems to mull over, or puzzles to solve, I seem to do it best away from my familiar haunts. There's something peaceful about these hills and this inn. Joe serves good food, good wine and good company. Unless I'm in the mood for solitude. Then he provides that, too.''

"I guess you can't ask for more." She played with the rim of her glass before looking at him. "So, what are you mulling over tonight?''

"I just thought it would be a nice change.''

"For me? Or for you?''

"For both of us.''

She continued staring at him. "You're not a very convincing liar, Micah.''

He managed a wicked grin that had her heart tripping over itself. "And here I thought I was doing so well."

He seemed almost relieved when the waitress returned with their salads. A short time later, while Prudence tucked into a seafood pasta, he cut off a piece of perfectly broiled prime rib and chewed woodenly.

When his cell phone rang, he excused himself and walked to a secluded section of the room before answering it. For long minutes he listened, then rang off and made another call.

When he heard Allen Street's voice, he said without preamble, "Micah Lassiter. Your daughter's here with me in a safe place. There's been no harm done to her, but her car was deliberately tampered with, causing her brakes to fail. The report is being faxed to you as we speak. The next move is up to you. I say it's time you told her the truth and asked her to fly home to Seattle."

The voice on the other end was brusque. "My thought exactly. I'll confer with my people and get back to you. In the meantime, keep her with you."

"For how long?"

"Until I say otherwise. Can you invent an excuse to stay in her apartment?"

"If I have to."

"You have no choice. Lassiter, I don't want her alone for a single minute. Is that clear?"

"Perfectly."

There was a long, deep sigh. "Thank you."

Micah disconnected and glanced across the room. Allen Street didn't know what he was asking of him. This could prove to be the longest night of his life.

He headed back to the booth, mentally shifting gears. This time he was determined to be a better liar.

His smile was quick and easy. "Just a minor adjustment needed to your braking system. Your car should be good as new in the morning."

Pru couldn't hide her relief. "Oh, that's good news." She arched an eyebrow. "I had no idea the mechanics worked this late."

Micah picked up his glass and stared into the pale wine with a frown. When he lifted his head, the rogue's smile was back. "I guess it's all in who you know."

"Tired?" Micah maneuvered the car around the curving ribbon of road, before glancing at Pru beside him.

She nodded. "A little. It's been a long day."

"If you'd like to close your eyes, I won't mind."

She shook her head. "I've never been able to sleep in a car. I have this crazy need to keep my eyes on the road, even when I'm not driving."

"All right. You watch the road and I'll close my eyes."

That had her laughing. "Now I know I'm not going to sleep."

"Coward."

She studied the lights of houses off in the distance. "I'm glad we got out of the city. I like your friend's inn."

"I'm glad. Tell everyone you know. Joe needs the business."

"It's funny." She turned to watch him as he smoothly handled the wheel. "I've been here a year now, and have barely been out of Georgetown."

"You're missing a lot of beautiful countryside."

"I know." She turned to study the lighted windows of shops and houses as they passed through a little town. "There's so much history in this part of the country. I visited some of the historic battlefields when I first came here, and I was moved to tears."

"Remind me to take you on a walking tour. You can feel the presence of all those soldiers. Sometimes they brush up against you as you pass."

"You surprise me." She studied his profile.

Margot had been right. He was so rugged, so handsome, he took her breath away. "I didn't expect
someone like you to believe in spirits."

"Someone like me?"

She smiled. "You strike me as a realist."

"I am. And trust me, the spirits on those battlefields are real."

At the intensity of his words, she felt a shiver
along her spine. It was, she realized, another side
to the very complicated Micah Lassiter. One he'd
managed to keep carefully hidden.

As they drew closer to the city, they could see
the lights of the Capitol dome and the Washington
Monument. While Micah maneuvered through traffic, Pru found herself thinking how pleasant these
past few hours had been. She hated to have them
come to an end.

In Georgetown, Micah turned into their street
and parked in the garage. By the time he stepped
out of the car, his gaze had already swept every
darkened corner of the structure, and had spotted
his operative lurking on the far side, as he'd been
ordered.

Inside the apartment building, Pru dug out her
key and opened the door, then turned to Micah
with a puzzled frown. "My alarm is off. I'd have
sworn I set it when I left this morning."

"Stay here." He strode across the foyer and

walked through every room of her apartment before returning. Not that he expected to find anyone. His operatives had done a thorough search while he and Pru were at dinner. It had been Micah who had ordered her alarm turned off. It was all part of his plan to keep his word to her father.

"There's nobody here, and nothing seems out of place. Are you sure you set the alarm?"

She shook her head. "I can't be absolutely certain. But it's part of my routine when I'm leaving."

"All right. So you may or may not have set it this morning. At any rate—" he pointed to the alarm "—set it now."

"Before you leave?"

He merely smiled. "I'm not leaving."

He could see the warring of emotions in her expressive eyes. On the one hand she didn't want to face the night alone. Still, she felt a trace of annoyance at his take-charge attitude. This was, after all, her private space, which he was now invading.

She crossed her arms over her chest and made a feeble attempt to protest. "Don't I have something to say about this?"

He shook his head. And though he was still smiling, Pru could hear the thread of steel in his voice. "Sorry. Like it or not, I'm staying the night.

Don't forget. Security is my business. Why not take advantage of that?''

She turned away, hoping he wouldn't hear the relief in her voice. ''I hope you don't mind sleeping on the sofa.''

Pru lay in bed listening to the muffled sounds of the night. How could she possibly sleep knowing Micah was in the next room? It had been bad enough when he'd been just across the hall. But at least they'd each had their own space. Now he was here. Just a door away. And the thought of going to him, of asking him to hold her, was almost too tempting to resist.

She rolled to her side and tried to block the memory of his kiss. But there was no turning off her mind. Even in the darkness, with her eyes tightly closed, she could see the way he had looked. It had been exciting to watch him struggle for control. To feel all that pent-up passion ready to explode.

And what an explosion. When he'd finally kissed her, she'd felt as though she was being swept up in something all-consuming. Helpless against the torrent of passion that flowed over her and carried her along until she was drowning in it.

She touched a hand to her heart. It was thundering. Just thinking about Micah's kiss had her struggling for breath.

She pulled the covers over her head and prayed for sleep.

Pru was having such a lovely dream. It was a hot summer day. She was driving her little sports car. The top was down, the wind whipping her hair as she maneuvered the sharp curves along the Virginia highway. She hadn't a care in the world. It was the most wonderful feeling to be free. Suddenly the car speeded up. She touched the brakes, but nothing happened. She clutched the wheel and felt the car hurtling through space.

Somewhere in the night, brakes screeched and tires squealed.

Pru sat up in bed shivering violently. It took her a moment to realize that it had all been a dream.

She glanced at the clock. She'd been asleep for more than two hours. How would she ever get back to sleep now?

She stepped out of bed and was halfway across the bedroom before she remembered that Micah was asleep in the next room. It was comforting to know she wasn't alone. Comforting and...exhilarating.

He was here. In her space. Asleep and unguarded. For the first time since they'd met, she would be free to study him without his knowledge.

She opened the door softly and started across the floor.

The great room was in darkness. She glanced at the sofa and could see the darker mound of pillows and blankets. She tiptoed close and was just about to peer down when she caught sight of a shadowy figure standing in front of the French doors. She tried to scream but her throat was so constricted it came out as a croak.

The figure was across the room and hauling her into his arms before she could recover.

"Micah." His name came out in a whoosh of air.

"Sorry." His breath was warm against her cheek. "I didn't mean to startle you."

"You didn't startle me." She struggled for air, but it was so hard to breathe when he was holding her like this. "You absolutely terrified me."

He ought to step back and give her some space. But he couldn't seem to let go of her. "You shouldn't come creeping up on a guy like that."

"The last I looked, this was my place." Her voice sounded breathless in her own ears. But she couldn't tell if it was because of fear or guilt. After all, she had been hoping to catch him unaware, and was instead caught in her own trap. "You're the one creeping around, Micah."

"I wasn't creeping around. I was…" Standing guard, he thought. Ready to slay any dragons that dared to threaten his princess while she slept in her ivory tower. Aloud he said, "Admiring the garden."

"In the dark?" Her head came up, her mouth brushing his jaw.

He absorbed a rush of heat and felt his pulse begin to speed up. "It's beautiful by moonlight." His voice lowered. "And so are you." He knew he couldn't go on holding her like this without putting his hands on her. His mouth on hers. And so he lowered his hands to his sides and clenched them into fists to keep from touching her.

He studied the white silk slip that barely covered her from torso to hip. "Is that all you wear to bed?"

She was grateful for the darkness. She hoped it would give her courage. "I didn't realize I'd have an audience."

The sight of her had him thinking about devouring her, inch by glorious inch. He started to turn away. "Maybe you'd better get a robe."

She stopped him with a hand to his arm. Just a touch, but she felt him flinch. "Why, Micah?" She could hear the tremor in her voice, but she was determined to put up a brave front. "Are you afraid to see me like this?"

"Afraid?" His throat was dry as dust. "In my line of work I've seen dozens of women wearing less than that. Now, why don't you do whatever it was you came out here to do and let me get back to what I was doing."

"That's right. I'd forgotten." She gave him a long, sweeping look, noting the fact that he was fully dressed right down to his shoes, and the bedding on the sofa wasn't even mussed. "You were busy watching the garden, I believe."

Her voice was taunting him. Whispering over his senses. Making him want what he had no right to.

"Don't play games with me, Pru. I'm in no mood."

"Just what is your mood, Micah?" She took a step closer, forcing him to hold himself perfectly still. If he so much as breathed too hard, he'd feel the brush of her breasts against his chest.

"My mood is pretty dark. So don't push."

"You mean like this?" She brought her hand to his chest. Just a touch of her fingertips, but he could feel it go straight to his loins.

"You're playing with fire, Pru." He closed a hand around her wrist.

"Maybe I like the heat." She brought her other

hand to his cheek and stood on tiptoe to brush her mouth over his.

He tensed, preparing himself for the firestorm to come. If he gave in now, they would both be lost. "Believe me, you won't like getting burned."

"Is that what you're afraid of? Getting burned?" She pressed closer, determined to break through that iron will. "You want me, Micah. You know you do."

"Maybe." His eyes narrowed. "But I don't always get what I want."

"You can, if you're honest enough to admit to it."

"I see. It's honesty you're looking for. And all along, I thought you were just looking for a few thrills."

She tossed her head. "Don't mince words. I want you, Micah."

"You don't even know me. Or what I'm doing here. And once you do, you'll regret ever having said that."

"There will be no regrets. I don't care who or what you are. I only know that I've never wanted anyone the way I want you. I want you to make love with me. Kiss me, Micah. Quick."

He caught her roughly by the shoulders, intent on saving her from herself. But the minute his hands were on her, he knew he'd lost the battle.

In the darkness he could see the glint of moonlight in her eyes. Eyes fixed on him with such hunger. They spoke to a hunger deep inside him.

He lowered his mouth to hers. Against her lips he whispered, "God knows I never meant this to happen, Pru. But unless you tell me right this minute that you've changed your mind, there'll be no stopping it."

"I don't want you to stop, Micah." Her voice was rough with need. "I want you. I want this as much as you do."

Chapter 11

There was no longer any way Micah could hold back. He'd tried heroically to do the right thing. But he was a mere man, desperate for this woman in his arms.

His mouth was on hers, kissing her with all the passion and feeling that had been building all these long, lonely nights. His hands moved over her, setting off sparks wherever they touched. And now, at last, they were free to touch her everywhere.

The thin silk was no barrier. It only added to her allure. He slid one narrow strap from her shoulder, then lowered his mouth to follow the trail until she gasped with pleasure.

Her skin, milk-white and soft as cream, carried the scent of spring flowers. As he tasted her, he breathed in the fragrance, filling himself with her. In the years to come, he knew, he would never again be able to smell spring without thinking of her. Of this. She'd taken over his life, his heart and soul, completely.

The hem of her slip rode high on her thigh. It was deeply arousing to feel the softness of silk, and the smooth texture of her flesh beneath. Though he was tempted to take her hard and fast, he resisted. He'd waited too long. Wanted too desperately. And now that he was free to have all that he wanted, he would savor the moment. She was, with all her shy, sweet alluring ways, a wonderful banquet of delights.

He lingered over her lips, drawing out the kiss until he heard her sigh with impatience and clutch at his waist. And still the kiss spun on and on, until, hungry for more, he ran soft, nibbling kisses along the smooth column of her throat.

Pru arched her neck, loving the feel of his mouth on her skin. She'd never known a man's kiss could bring such pleasure. There was a quiet intensity in him. In every move he made. Everything he did. He made her feel like a special gift to be opened. And with each touch, each kiss, she could feel herself opening more.

His fingertips stroked, soothed, and she began to relax in his arms until they suddenly found her. Her eyes went wide with shock as he took her up and over. Shuddering, she nearly collapsed in his arms. In one smooth motion he scooped her up and carried her to the sofa, where he lay her down among the blankets. And all the while his mouth lingered on hers until she wanted to beg for more.

"Micah." She pulled back, her eyes glazed.

"I warned you, Pru." His mouth returned to hers, while his body pressed her deeper into the cushions. "Don't ask me to stop now."

"I wasn't..." She struggled for breath. Her heart was pounding, but whether from excitement or fear, she wasn't sure. "I wouldn't ask you that. Please don't stop."

He chuckled against her skin. He couldn't if he'd wanted to. He was already in over his head, tumbling faster and faster into a deep, dark cavern. And taking her down with him.

Their breathing was ragged, their heartbeats erratic. Moonlight spilled through the French doors, gilding her flesh, turning her hair to flame. His hands fisted in it as he kissed her until they were both breathless.

Desperate to touch him, she tore at his shirt until he'd managed to shed it, along with the rest of his clothes. She was humming with pleasure when at last she was free to run her fingertips across his hair-roughened chest and revel in the feel of those perfectly toned muscles beneath her palms.

She thought, because he was fully aroused, that he would take her, and end this terrible need. But he had other plans.

His hands, those incredibly strong hands, moved over her with such care. His rough fingertips felt like heaven against the silkiness of her flesh. She'd never known a man to treat her with such care. As though she were some fragile piece of glass that might shatter at any moment in his hands.

Just as she began to relax in his arms, he lowered his mouth to burn a trail of fire down her body, unlocking new secrets. She tensed, knowing she had never experienced such a dark side of passion before. But with Micah leading the way, she was helpless to do more than follow.

Her breathing grew labored. The air felt hot, clogging her lungs, pearling her flesh. When he took her on a dizzying upward spiral, she could do nothing more than clutch the blanket while her body shuddered, before going limp.

"Micah."

"This was how I've dreamed of you, Pru." In the moonlight his eyes were hot and fierce as he tore away the silk. "Your hair wild and loose. Your spirit free. The taste of you so sweet. So sweet." He ran his mouth across her throat, over her breasts, until she sobbed out his name and fisted a hand in his hair. "And mine. If only for tonight, all mine."

Desperate, she wrapped herself around him, drawing him in. He struggled to hold back, but there was a beast inside him, struggling for freedom. He plunged himself inside her and heard her sudden cry. For one heart-stopping moment he hesitated. Then she whispered his name. Just one breathy whisper, but he could feel himself drowning in her and he knew he never wanted to surface.

When he began moving, she matched his rhythm, his strength, until they were moving together, racing toward a distant peak.

He breathed her in, filling himself with her until she seemed to be in every part of him. His heart. His lungs. His very soul.

His, he thought with a fierceness that bordered on insanity. Only his.

He breathed her name against her mouth as they took each other over the top. And soared to the star-filled heavens.

Micah lay on the sofa, watching the way the thin morning light played over the woman in his arms.

He'd always loved sunlight. Until today. Right now he'd give everything he had to hold it at bay, so that he could stay just like this for a few hours more. Holding Pru close to his heart. Watching her sleep as peacefully as a child. He knew that once she woke, their little idyll would be over. He would have to go back to being her silent protector, holding her at arm's length until the threat to her safety was over. And once it was, they'd go their separate ways. There was no place in her world for him. And certainly no place in his world for a woman like Pru.

That knowledge left a bitter taste in his mouth. Still, if they had nothing more, at least they'd had the night. She'd been amazing. Sweet. Funny. Sexy. And so trusting. It pleased him to know that he'd taken her to places she'd never been before. She'd gone with him willingly and with such abandon. They'd both been dazzled by her response.

She stirred and he watched as her lashes fluttered, then opened. He found himself drowning in those wide, trusting eyes. If only they could always be so trusting.

"Good morning, Micah." She wrapped her arms around his neck and pressed her lips to his.

At once he felt the jolt and wondered how he would be able to go on living without this. It was almost worse, knowing he'd be consigned to hell now that he'd had a taste of heaven. But he had nobody to blame but himself. He'd walked into this with his eyes wide open. Pru, on the other hand, had no idea what a hornet's nest she'd uncovered. But she would soon enough. And when she did, she would hate him.

"'Morning." He lingered over her mouth for a moment, then abruptly sat up and began disentangling himself from her.

She couldn't hide her disappointment. "Where are you going?"

"To my apartment to shower and dress." He turned away and picked up his discarded shirt, leaving it unbuttoned as he drew it on.

"Do you have to go right away?"

He walked past her and headed toward the foyer. "I'm afraid so."

"Micah." He was almost at the door when she stopped him with a hand on his arm.

The heat was growing. Threatening to steal his very breath. He knew if he turned toward her, he'd be lost. "You're going to be late for work, Pru."

"That's all right. They don't pay me anyway." She wrapped her arms around his waist and pressed her mouth to his back. "I guess if I'm late just this once, I won't worry about being fired."

"Pru…" He turned. That was his first mistake. His second was putting his hands on her shoulders, to draw her away. Everything after that seemed to happen in slow motion. The way she offered her lips. The way she pressed that perfect body against his. He was drowning in her again. And not even trying to resist.

Against her mouth he murmured, "I guess…as long as you have time…"

They never even made it to the sofa before taking each other on a wild, dizzying ride.

"I don't understand why they couldn't return my car today." Pru followed Micah from the parking garage to her apartment and fumbled with her key.

"They said there were a few things they wanted to check first." After speaking with Allen Street, Micah had persuaded him that Pru was better off riding with him than being alone in her flashy little convertible. For once, her father had agreed. "It ought to be ready in a day or two."

"Good." Pru touched a finger to his cheek. "Not that I don't enjoy riding with you, Micah. But I've come to enjoy a certain freedom here in Georgetown that I never had before. That's hard to give up."

He winced as he took the key from her hand and opened her door. Nothing like twisting the knife a little deeper.

"About dinner, Micah. I was thinking—"

She gave a little yelp as he tugged her back, placing himself in front of her.

"What is it?" She watched as he dropped to the floor and picked up something before straightening.

"I left this in the doorway this morning when we left your apartment." He held up a length of thread so clear as to be almost invisible. "The fact that it's been disturbed means someone has been in here. Stay here." His tone was pure ice. And though she'd never been issued a command in such a tone, she knew better than to argue.

After a thorough search of every room in her apartment, he returned and took her hand. "I want you to look around carefully and see if anything has been moved or taken."

"Micah. Are you joking? The alarm was on. How could anything be gone? If anyone was here, wouldn't they have set off the alarm?"

"To a professional, a security system like yours is a walk in the park. Now, humor me, Pru. Look around. Does anything seem out of place?"

She walked through the great room, her gaze sweeping the sofa, the bookshelves, the mantel. While she did, Micah was going through the rooms, checking the backs of pictures and lifting lamps to check their bases for any sign of electronic bugging.

He made a terse phone call, ordering his operatives to come at once and bring along their equipment.

Pru had never seen him this intense. To lighten his mood, she pressed a kiss to his cheek. He paused and gave her a long, lingering look before returning his attention to the objects on her desk.

Pru was just turning away when she paused beside her computer and frowned.

"What?" Micah walked up to stand next to her.

"I never close my laptop unless I'm taking it with me."

"You're sure?"

She nodded.

"Don't touch it."

"What do you mean, Micah? I could be mistaken."

"Always trust your first instincts. Come on." Without another word, Micah caught her hand and led her out the door.

She had no chance to ask questions as he pulled her across the hall. Once there, he opened his door and stood aside until she'd entered Professor Loring's apartment.

There were a million questions racing through Pru's mind. But Micah gave her no chance to ask them as he leaned against the closed door and pulled a cell phone from his pocket.

After dialing, he waited with a hiss of impatience before saying, "Allen. Micah Lassiter here. Our guy knows where Pru lives." He listened a moment, then nodded. "I'll put her on the phone now and leave it to you to explain why she has to leave here and fly home to Seattle at once."

"What are you...? Micah, what is this all about?"

As he handed over the phone, he saw Pru's eyes narrow, and wished he had time to explain. But thanks to one clever stalker, time had just run out.

Chapter 12

"Dad?" Pru couldn't hide the shock she was feeling. "Why are you...? How do you know Micah Lassiter?"

Micah crossed his arms over his chest, watching and listening in stony silence.

At her father's words, her head came up. "I see. And you didn't think you ought to bother me with such...unpleasant details as a madman making threats, and the fact that you'd hired a personal bodyguard to keep me safe."

The voice on the other end grew louder.

Her eyes narrowed. "You didn't want to what? Admit that you'd once again yanked away my free-

dom? Or were you afraid the news might frighten
me? Send me running like a little mouse back into
my hole? Is that what you're saying? Do you think
I'm so fragile, so helpless I might fall apart if I'm
trusted with the truth?''

There was another angry volley of words, and
then her father gave a curt command.

Without a word Pru handed the phone to Micah.
He watched as she stormed across the room and
tore open the door.

He muttered into the phone, ''Allen, I think you
have a problem.''

The voice on the other end sounded suddenly
weary. ''No, Lassiter, it's your problem. Do whatever you have to. But see that my daughter is out
of that apartment and into someplace safe within
the hour. Call and let me know where you are. I'm
sending my private plane to bring her back here
immediately.''

Micah was already starting across the hall,
barely able to stop the door before it was slammed
in his face. As he shoved it open and stepped inside, he caught sight of Pru heading toward her
bedroom.

Into the phone he muttered, ''Thanks for the
cushy assignment, Allen. I'll report back later.''

He dropped the phone in his pocket and put a
hip against the door, which he knew would be

locked. It took only one quick shove to break through. As expected, Pru was standing across the room, her face as angry as a thundercloud.

"You were hired by my father." Her voice trembled with fury. "All this time, I thought you were trying to get close to me for myself, and you were working for my father."

"Pru, listen to me...."

He started toward her, but she kept backing up until she bumped into the wall.

"No. You listen to me. All my life I've had to deal with this. My father keeping me under lock and key. Private schools. The same small circle of friends. Even my occasional dates approved by and chosen by my father. I had to move across the country to make a life for myself. My life, Micah."

Her eyes, he realized, were a little too bright. She was fighting tears. He didn't know what he'd do if she started crying. But though he longed to offer her comfort, all he could do was let her unload on him.

"I know it was stupid. I let the Vandevere sisters talk me into believing something I knew was too good to be true. But it isn't their fault. It's mine. I was so silly, so stupid. I wanted romance. And all you wanted was to do your job."

"Pru, this isn't about—"

She held up a hand to stop him. "Oh, I must

look like such a fool. Some love-starved female who can't even get a man unless he's bought and paid for by her rich daddy.''

''You know that isn't—''

Her head snapped up. ''You're working for my father. He bought and paid for you. And that's the only reason you're here. Can you deny that?''

''No.'' He clenched his hands at his sides in impotent fury.

The silence was deafening.

''Well.'' She blinked hard. She would not cry. She was already deeply humiliated. She wouldn't make it worse. Not in front of this man. ''You can tell my father that I'm not going back to Seattle. This is my home now, and I'll damn well live where I please.''

''It won't be forever, Pru. It's just until we catch...''

She pressed her hands to her ears and closed her eyes, as if to shut him out. ''Go away, Micah. I'm not leaving. And you can't make me.''

''All right.'' He took a step closer. ''If you're going to act like a child, that's how I'll have to treat you.''

''What are you...?'' She shrank from his touch, but he was stronger and quicker.

In one smooth motion he picked her up and tossed her over his shoulder like a sack of grain.

"Put me down." She pounded on his back, but he ignored her blows as though they were nothing more than powder puffs.

"Micah." She was shouting now, kicking her feet until he closed one big hand around her ankles to keep them still.

On the way out he snatched up her purse. At the door he paused long enough to set the alarm and turn the key in the lock. Then he strode past Octavia and Odelia Vandevere, who were too startled to do more than stare in openmouthed surprise, and into the garage, where he deposited Pru in his car. She made one desperate attempt to break free, but he snagged her wrist and held her while he turned on the ignition.

As he backed out of the garage and waited for traffic to clear, he shot her a look. "Fasten your seat belt."

"You mean you trust me to handle such a complicated chore?" Her voice was pure ice. "I thought that's what my father hired you to do for me."

"Suit yourself." He leaned over and fastened her seat belt. As he did, his hand brushed the underside of her breast.

Once again she shrank from his touch.

He swore under his breath as he pulled into traffic. His hands on the wheel were none too steady.

Temper, he knew. It had nothing at all to do with the fact that whatever feelings he might have for Prudence Street were now off limits for good.

Micah turned his car into the quiet residential street, past the line of sprawling old houses with their neatly manicured lawns. When he turned into the driveway of his mother's house, he noted glumly that Bren's car was there, as well as Cam's. Just his luck. If he weren't so angry, he'd probably feel at least a twinge of sympathy for the poor woman who was about to meet, and be over-whelmed by, most of his family, all in one big bite.

"Where are we?" Pru was reeling from the twists and turns in traffic Micah had taken to avoid being followed.

"My mother's place." He walked around the car and held her door.

"Why are we here?"

"You can't stay in your apartment. And you seem hell-bent on not returning to Seattle."

"I'll take a hotel room."

"Not tonight." He took her arm and led her up the steps of the front porch before opening the door. She had no choice but to step inside. Almost at once she heard the sound of voices and laughter coming from the back of the house.

"Sounds like everyone's in the kitchen." He

pointed. "That's where they can usually be found."

"Who is everyone?"

"My family. Or most of them." He led the way and threw open the door to the kitchen.

"Well, look who blew in. No surprise here," Bren called from across the room. "You always seem to make it just in time for dinner, Micah."

"Thanks for that warm greeting, little sis." Micah stepped aside and drew Prudence into the room. "Everyone, this is Prudence Street. Pru, this is my mother, Kate, and my grandfather, Kieran. My sister, Bren, and my brother Cam."

Suddenly overcome with shyness, Pru shook Kate's hand and merely nodded a greeting to the others.

"Well, now. Come in, Prudence." Kate gave her a welcoming smile before returning her attention to something on the stove. "Dinner will be ready in just a little while. I hope you and Micah can stay."

"We wouldn't miss it." Micah reached over his mother's shoulder to help himself to a biscuit, which he broke in half before devouring. "In fact, I was wondering if it would be all right if we spent the night."

Kate barely paused in her work before nodding.

"That's not a problem. Prudence can have Bren's room. And you can have your old room."

Pru was already shaking her head in refusal. "I couldn't possibly take your daughter's room, Mrs. Lassiter."

"I don't sleep here anymore." Bren carried a tray of steaming vegetables toward the dining room.

"Bren has her own place." Cam picked up a whistling kettle and poured boiling water into a teapot. "As a matter of fact, so does Micah." He turned to his brother. "So why are you staying here tonight?"

Micah slapped his shoulder. "That's for me to know and you to find out, little brother."

"Well, I know it can't be because you forgot to pay your electric bill. Not after that hefty check you got from—" Cam felt the elbow in his ribs and nearly dropped the kettle. "Hey." Then his head whipped around and he studied Pru more carefully.

His reaction wasn't lost on her. Though no one had said a word, it was obvious that they all knew who she was. Her chin came up a fraction, as though bracing for questions.

Instead, Kieran fixed his youngest grandson with a fierce look and said, "Help your sister in the other room, Cam."

"Yes, sir."

Kieran shot a look at Micah. "You might want to lend a hand, too. The rest of us have put in a full day."

"Sure. I've just been twiddling my thumbs." With a grin Micah picked up a platter of roast beef and headed for the dining room.

"Well." Kieran turned to Pru. "Welcome to our home, lass. Come along now. Dinner is ready."

Like a gallant old gentleman, Kieran held the door for his daughter-in-law, Kate, and their guest, and directed Pru to sit beside Micah at the long dining-room table, while he took his place at one end, with Kate at the other.

As if by silent command, as soon as they were seated, they reached out their hands to one another. Pru felt her hand caught and held by Micah on one side and by Kieran on the other.

The old man's voice was rich with the music of Ireland as he said, "Bless this food. And this family. Not only those of us gathered here, but those who are here in spirit. Bless Donovan, wherever he may be at the moment. And Riordan, who watches over us all."

The others murmured "Amen" before releasing hands and passing the food.

Pru felt more than a little staggered. She hadn't linked hands in prayer since she'd been a little girl.

And dinner in her father's home in Seattle had never been like this. For one thing, there was such a variety of food for a simple family meal. Slow-cooked roast beef swimming in mushroom gravy. Mashed potatoes. Green beans. A spinach soufflé. Rolls and butter. A pot of tea, and two frosty pitchers of milk.

Besides the abundance of food, there was the conversation. Each time someone spoke, it seemed that every other member of the family had an opinion on the subject.

"I met the sweetest young woman today." Kate buttered a roll and helped herself to beef before turning to Pru. "I have a law office in the District."

"She calls it a law office," Cam said with a smile. "But it's really a war zone."

"You ought to know." Micah smiled at Pru, who had been swiveling her head from one to the other, trying to follow the various threads of the conversation. "Cam takes on the desperate cases that nobody else wants to handle. He and Mom have become quite the team, working for the downtrodden of this world."

Despite the teasing, Pru could hear the note of affection in his tone. She glanced over at Kate. "Micah told me you're a family advocate."

"Someone has to be." Kate passed the platter of beef to her son. "What do you do, Prudence?"

She ducked her head when she realized everyone was looking at her. It was something she'd always done whenever she found herself the center of attention. "I work at the Children's Village."

"You do? How grand." Kate gave her a big smile. "I've sent clients there."

"Then you know Margot Jamison, the director."

"Very well. How is Margot?"

"She's…fine." Pru moved the food around her plate, hoping someone would draw the attention away from her.

Taking pity on her, Micah turned to his mother. "You started to tell us about the sweet woman you met."

"Oh yes." Kate launched into a story of the young mother and her three children who had come to her office for help. "They hadn't had breakfast or lunch, and all I had in my little office fridge was an egg-salad sandwich, which I promptly cut into small bites and passed around. Poor things. They acted like I'd just given them a pile of gold."

When Pru finally glanced up, she saw Micah look over and wink. Her heart took a hard, quick bounce before settling down to its natural rhythm.

While the conversation swirled around her, she reminded herself that she was still furious with him. One kind act didn't erase that he'd been lying since the day she'd met him. And she would never, ever trust him again.

They lingered over dinner for more than two hours. Dessert looked simple enough. A gelatin layered with slices of fresh fruit, and a plate of coconut-apricot bars.

After one bite, Pru looked up in surprise. "Oh, these are wonderful. Did you bake them, Mrs. Lassiter?"

"It's Kate, dear. And I haven't baked in years. Kieran does all the baking and cooking in this house."

Pru looked down, knowing her cheeks were flushed. "They're delicious, Mr. Lassiter."

"Kieran," he corrected. "Or better yet, just call me Pop. That's what everyone else calls me."

"I'd love your recipe...sir." She simply couldn't bring herself to call him by name.

"I'll see that you get it." He held up the fine china teapot. "How about some tea, Prudence?"

"Thank you." She waited while he poured, then sat back, enjoying her tea and a second helping of dessert while the conversation flowed around her.

"...of course, I'm still getting my feet wet, try-

ing to find my way around all those hallways and
meeting rooms.'' Bren gave a self-deprecating
grin, so like Micah's. ''But I've already been assigned a committee.''

''Oh, that's wonderful, Bren.'' Kate set down
her tea. ''I just know you're going to do great
things in Congress.''

''Congress?'' Pru's eyes widened. ''Of course.
That's why you look so familiar. You were just
elected to Congress.'' She turned to Micah. ''Why
didn't you tell me your sister was Congresswoman
Mary Brendan Lassiter?''

He shrugged. ''I figured sooner or later Bren
would let you in on it.'' He grinned at his sister
across the table. ''These days she tells anybody
who'll listen. I've known her to even stop strangers
in the mall to tell them who she is.''

''I've had to learn to blow my own horn,'' Bren
said with a laugh. ''Heaven knows my brothers are
so tight-lipped about their lives, if it were up to
them, nobody would have even known I was in the
congressional race until it was over.''

''All part of the training.'' Cam drained his
milk. ''Can you imagine our big brother Donovan
ever talking about his CIA jobs?''

Pru gasped. ''You have a brother in the CIA?''

Micah shook his head. ''Pure speculation on our
part. Donovan never talks about it. In fact, we

don't even know where he is. He calls from time to time, on a secure line, to tell us he's alive. That's about it.''

Pru glanced at Kate. ''How can you bear not knowing?''

Kate gave her a gentle smile. ''It's always hard letting children leave the nest.'' She turned to include Micah. ''Even those we know about. But I have confidence that I raised them to handle whatever life throws their way.''

Prudence fell silent, thinking about her own father, and the way she'd had to fight for even the most basic freedoms.

Kate pushed away from the table. ''That was a lovely dinner, Kieran. But now I have some paperwork to see to. I'll say good night.'' She paused beside Pru's chair. ''Micah will show you Bren's room. I'm sure you'll be happy to know that because she was the only girl, she got her own bathroom.''

''Thank you, Mrs....thank you, Kate. It's kind of you to take in a stranger.''

''You're hardly a stranger, Prudence. Not if you're here with my son.'' She brushed a kiss on Micah's cheek, then kissed her other children and her father-in-law before heading off to her bedroom.

When she was gone, Cam said, ''Mom's got

way too much paperwork. What she needs is some help in that office.''

''Then why don't you hire some?'' Micah drained his tea.

''Easier said than done. Do you know what it would take to persuade someone to work in that part of town? And even if we could, they'd want a fortune.''

''Then pay it. Mom deserves to relax when she comes home at night.''

Cam nodded. ''I never understood just how much work she'd taken on until I started taking some of her cases.''

Micah turned to Pru. ''Cam works part-time in one of the biggest law firms in the city, billing enough hours so he can afford to take on some pro bono cases that nobody else will touch.''

''Why won't anyone else touch them?''

Cam started gathering up the dishes. ''They're considered hopeless. Guys in prison, usually, who've been through all their appeals. Most of them come through Mom's office. She just has a way of ferreting out the ones who got a bad deal and deserve another look.''

''Do you ever get them a new trial?''

''Now and again.'' Cam turned to Micah. ''You going to sit there, or get off your duff and lend a hand?''

"I guess I could help. I'll load the dishwasher and you can do the pots and pans."

"No way." Cam started toward the kitchen with an armload of dishes. "I'll load the washer. You do the pots and pans."

"Wait a minute…" Micah began gathering up dishes in haste before dashing from the room.

"I can help, too." Pru started up until Kieran put a hand on her arm.

"You may as well relax. There's going to be a war in the kitchen in a few minutes."

"A war?" She looked at Bren with alarm.

"Just a minor scuffle." Bren laughed. "Which Pop will be more than happy to break up."

"They still fight? At their age?" Pru looked absolutely horrified at the sounds coming from the kitchen.

Just then Kieran pushed away from the table and stormed into the other room.

At the look on Pru's face, Bren leaned over and patted her hand. "It's just horseplay. But with guys, it's so easy to get out of hand. So Pop will order the usual punishment."

"Punishment? For grown men? He can do that?"

"Uh-huh. Pop rules this roost." Bren started laughing harder when the door slammed and the voices faded. "It's just begun. Come on. You and

I can finish the dishes and watch the entertainment through the window.''

In the kitchen, Bren led Pru to the window, where they saw Cam and Micah struggling for control of the basketball. Micah blocked, Cam dropped the ball, and Micah scooped it up and into the basket for a clean shot. Seconds later, Cam tossed the ball. It rimmed the net, and fell without going in. Micah was on him at once, dribbling the ball and scoring again.

Bren turned on the taps and started washing the roasting pan. ''If you'd like to load the rest of those dishes, we'll be finished long before the battle of the hoops has ended.''

''Do they ever come to blows?'' Pru paused a moment to watch a shoving match going on outside.

''Occasionally. But there's rarely much bloodshed.'' Pru turned pale and Bren dropped an arm around her shoulders. ''Hey, we're family. We may fight a bit, but we always make up.''

''That's a relief.'' Pru tore her gaze from the antics outside and concentrated on the dishes.

''Don't you have any brothers or sisters to fight with, Pru?''

The young woman shook her head. ''I always thought I'd like to have a few siblings. But seeing that…'' She nodded toward the backyard and gave a little shudder. ''I'm not so sure.''

Bren dried the roasting pan and put it in a cupboard. ''I've spent a lifetime cursing the fates that gave me brothers. But the truth is, I don't know what I'd do without them.''

By the time she and Bren had finished up in the kitchen, the two brothers were walking through the doorway, arms around each other's shoulders. Both of them were layered with sweat and laughing hysterically.

''Good game,'' Micah said.

''Yeah. And we managed to avoid the dishes, too.'' Cam swatted his sister's rear and was rewarded with a damp dish towel in the face.

Across the room Pru watched in amazement.

Micah leaned close to his sister and whispered, ''You wouldn't happen to have any nightclothes left up in your room, would you?''

''I might. Just some old stuff left over from college. Why?''

''Pru and I left in a bit of a hurry.''

Bren turned to their houseguest. ''Prudence, why don't I show you my room.'' As she and Pru started out of the kitchen, she noticed Micah trailing behind. She shot him a look. ''Where do you think you're going?''

He merely smiled. "Don't mind me. I'm just the bodyguard."

"Some bodyguard." She put an arm around Pru's shoulder and said in a loud voice, "If he doesn't soon shower, he won't have to use his muscle to fend off attackers. All he'll have to do is threaten to get close enough to smell all that sweat and they'll run the other way."

Despite her earlier anger, Pru couldn't help laughing. The barbs being passed around were simply priceless.

When she stepped into Bren's cozy room, she felt a little of the day's tension begin to slip away.

She glanced at the framed photo on the wall, of a handsome man in uniform surrounded by three little boys. In his arms was a little girl, looking at him with a look of absolute adoration. "Is that your father?"

Bren nodded. "Mom made each of us a memory book of old pictures, as well as newspaper accounts of his death." She opened a drawer and set an album on the desk. "I've added to it, so that all our family is chronicled. If you'd like to leaf through it, feel free."

"Thanks, Bren." Pru was grateful that Micah's sister seemed to sense her need to be alone.

After locating a nightshirt, and insisting that Pru

help herself to whatever clothes she might need in the morning, Bren bid her good-night.

An hour later, after luxuriating in a long hot shower, Prudence thumbed through the album and found herself marveling at what the Lassiter family had been through, and all that they'd done with their extraordinary lives.

At last she climbed between the covers and, for the first time since being rudely hauled out of her apartment, she had the time to mull over all that had happened.

Chapter 13

Just thinking about the fact that her father had hired Micah Lassiter as her bodyguard had Prudence punching a fist into her pillow. How could her own father have done such a thing without telling her? He claimed he was trying to spare her any unnecessary fear. Well, maybe that was so. But in the process he'd caused her the most appalling humiliation.

She thought about what Kate Lassiter had said tonight about letting go of her children. She trusted them. It galled Prudence to think that, even now, after years of college, and a graduate degree that would soon be added to her list of accomplishments, her father still wasn't willing to trust her to take care of herself. He hadn't even bothered to tell her about the danger she might be in. He simply hired others to look out for her.

What was worse, she had no idea the extent of the danger that threatened her. A madman, her father had said. One who felt targeted by her father and his company's software.

Thinking back to the e-mail incident, she understood now why Micah had reacted the way he had. Obviously the man and woman he'd called in to check her computer had been aware of the threat and had taken it very seriously. But whether they were employees of Micah, or of her father, she had no way of knowing.

Suddenly she remembered something else. The brakes on her car. Micah told her that it was a simple failure. What if it had been done deliberately? Those weren't just a few threatening words on a computer screen. It could have resulted in a tragedy if she had pulled into traffic before making the discovery that she had no brakes.

Her mind was reeling from the possibilities. No wonder Micah had taken her far away while her car was being checked. It hurt to realize he hadn't simply wanted to take her to a secluded restaurant for the sake of furthering their relationship.

Oh, how it hurt.

And then there was the fact that a stranger had broken into her apartment, had disarmed her security alarm and had looked at, even touched, her belongings. She felt naked. Vulnerable. Violated.

Though she wasn't aware of it, she curled up into a tight ball and pulled the blankets over her head, the way she had when she'd been a shy little girl trying to shut out the world.

Gradually sleep overtook her.

Kieran Lassiter poured himself a foamy mug of dark beer and started toward the stairs. This was his little treat to himself when the chores were finished and the day done. A mug of cold beer and the History Channel. Life didn't get much better than that.

As he passed through the great room, he caught sight of Micah in the big easy chair, the glow from the tip of a cigar gleaming red in the shadows.

"What're you doing sitting in the dark?"

"Relaxing." Micah drew in smoke and watched it curl over his head.

"Aren't you going up to bed?"

Micah shook his head. "Not tonight."

"You on duty?" He nodded toward the stairs. "Guarding the lass?"

"Yeah."

The old man perched on the edge of the footstool. "Is she in trouble?"

"Could be. There've been threats. And today someone got into her apartment."

"Did they take anything?"

"Not that we could see. My operatives will sweep it tonight to look for bugs. But even if it's clean, it's enough to know that someone was there, violating her space. I had to get her out of there."

"Why not your place?"

Micah shrugged. "For one thing, I may have been spotted by this guy. He tampered with her brakes in the parking lot of a store. If he'd stayed there to watch, he'd have seen us come out together. I figure if he can find her place, he can find mine, too."

"What's the other thing?"

Micah arched an eyebrow.

The old man smiled. "You said for one thing. What's the other?"

Micah winced. "She was so mad at me when she found out I'd been hired by her father, I figured it wouldn't be wise to be alone with her. She was liable to brain me with the nearest thing she could find and take off on her own."

Kieran chuckled. "Good move." He stood, holding the mug carefully so as not to spill a drop of his precious brew. "I'll say good night now."

"Good night, Pop."

Micah watched as his grandfather climbed the stairs. Then he closed his eyes a moment. It was true that he hadn't wanted to be alone with Pru. But not for the reason he gave Pop. The truth was, he wanted her so badly, he was no longer willing to trust himself.

Prudence awoke with a start and glanced at the bedside clock. She'd been asleep for several hours. The thought of the long night looming before her had her suddenly wide awake, her mind once again whirling with all that had happened.

A madman was on the loose. Her life could quite possibly be in danger. But none of that seemed real. What was real to her was that she'd made a total and complete fool of herself.

How was she going to face Micah?

Just thinking about the way she had set out to seduce him had her burying her face in her hands. No wonder he'd fought so hard to resist temptation. She'd thought he was just a reluctant lover. Now she realized he'd been trying to spare her exactly what she was now suffering. He'd known that sooner or later she would have to learn the truth. And when she did, she would not only hate him, but herself.

So why had he finally succumbed to her advances?

Micah Lassiter didn't strike her as the sort of man to violate that code of honor he wore so nobly. Maybe she'd caught him in a weak moment. Or maybe he'd wanted her as much as she'd wanted him.

The very thought of it had her heart giving a wild flutter.

He'd been the most amazing lover. There was no denying that he'd been as fully engaged as she. It had been, at least for that one special night, a dance which, though initiated by one, had been thoroughly enjoyed by two.

And so, here she was. In this strange place, with a houseful of strangers.

After the initial shock of his family, she'd had a grand time seeing Micah with them tonight. When he was around them he seemed softer somehow. More human. She loved the warm, easy way they interacted. The gentle gibes. The joking, teasing banter. The love and affection. It was there in their eyes for everyone to see.

And now, after studying Bren's album, she realized just what an amazing family they were. Talk about overachievers. No wonder her father had trusted Micah Lassiter to be her bodyguard.

Her bodyguard. The very word grated on her

nerves. It was so like Allen Street to think his precious little princess needed guarding.

She gritted her teeth, feeling the sting of anger and humiliation.

Too on edge to go back to sleep she slipped out of bed and crossed the room. She didn't think Kieran Lassiter would mind if she helped herself to a cup of his tea.

The stairs were cloaked in darkness. She used the banister to find her way. Once in the great room, there was a pool of moonlight to guide her to the kitchen.

She had her hand on the door when she saw something move in the shadows. Before she could scream, there was a hand on her mouth and a heaviness against her body, propelling her through the doorway and into the kitchen, which was quickly flooded with light.

When she realized it was Micah holding her, she mouthed his name, but no words came out. She had to stop, swallow and try again.

"Sorry." Micah released her and took a step back. "I figured I'd just let you go by without revealing myself. But when you saw me, I figured you'd scream and wake the household."

She drew in a shaky breath. "That was definitely my intention."

"I'm really sorry, Pru." He was trying not to

stare. But the sight of her in a faded Washington
Redskins shirt that hung to her knees seemed so
incongruous. Especially when he knew that de-
signer silk was much more her style. "I see Bren
gave you something to wear. Did you sleep at
all?"

"For a while." She couldn't tell if her trembling
was merely a reaction to shock, or because of the
look in Micah's eyes. "I thought I'd make myself
some tea."

"I'll have some, too." He turned toward a cupboard and took down two cups.

Grateful for something to do, Prudence filled the
kettle and set it on the stove, while Micah opened
a canister and brought out two tea bags.

When he set them in the cups, he couldn't help
chuckling. "If Pop saw us making our tea this way,
he'd be offended."

"Why?"

"It's the Irish in him. He believes that tea should
be steeped in a teapot, not in a cup."

"Has he always been such a courtly gentleman?"

"Gentleman." Micah thought about that a moment before nodding. "I suppose. Especially
around women. He adores my mother. He thought
she was the best thing that had ever happened to
his son. And he was really wild about Bren when

she was born. He spent so much time carrying her around in his arms my father worried that she'd never learn to walk. So I guess when it comes to the ladies, Kieran Lassiter is definitely a gentleman. But on the D.C. police force he was known as a tough cop who never backed away from a fight.''

''It's hard to imagine that sweet old man wearing a uniform and carrying a gun.'' She removed the kettle from the stove and filled the two cups with boiling water.

''Looks can be deceiving.'' Ignoring the big trestle table that dominated the other end of the kitchen, Micah led her to a padded window seat overlooking the backyard. ''Take that basketball hoop, for instance.'' He nodded toward the moonlight glinting off the backboard. ''Looks harmless enough, I suppose. But for all of my life it's been the place where all of us were sent to work off our aggression.''

She smiled and sipped her tea. ''I noticed. It seems to work.''

''Yeah.'' He leaned a hip against the wall while he drank his tea. ''There's just something about running back and forth making hoops that drains away the anger.''

He'd showered and changed into a pair of drawstring pants and a crewneck sweater in charcoal gray. On his feet were dark socks. Even here, with moonlight spilling through the window, he seemed to prefer to blend into the shadows. No wonder she hadn't seen him in the other room.

She glanced over. "May I ask you something?"

Though his smile remained, she thought she could feel him tense. "Sure. What would you like to know?"

"How did my father find you?"

"He asked around. One of his security agents used to work with me."

"In the Secret Service?"

He arched an eyebrow. "I see you've been doing a little digging."

"Bren offered me her family album." She set aside her tea. "I assume your family knows about me as well."

"Not much. Only what little they could overhear when your father came here. As you can imagine, I didn't volunteer anything more."

She nearly smiled before she caught herself. "What about Margot Jamison? And Professor Loring?"

"Nobody knew. This was between your father and me."

She let out a breath. "I'm glad. I wouldn't want to think I was the only one who'd been kept in the dark."

"I'm sorry about that, Pru."

"I know." She looked down at her hands. "Now that I've had time to think, I realize you had no choice but to do whatever my father told you. If I'm going to be angry with someone, it'll be Dad."

"Just remember that he did it because he loves you. He called you his most precious treasure."

"Oh yes. I know all about his pet phrases. His treasure. His princess. But he can't keep on treating me like a child, Micah. Other parents know how to let go. Look at your mother. It has to weigh heavily on her heart that she doesn't even know where your brother Donovan is living, or how he's living. But she's willing to trust his judgment."

Micah gave a wry laugh.

Her head came up. "What's so funny?"

"You'd have to know Donovan. He's always been a wild man. I don't think he ever really got over our dad's death. Either that, or there was a devil inside him. As for Mom trusting him, I'd say she has no choice. Donovan lives exactly as he pleases. Always has, always will."

"But at least she's come to terms with it. My father absolutely refuses to accept that I'm a woman now, with a life of my own. He still wants to treat me like his little girl."

Micah's voice was low as he emptied his cup and set it aside. "I don't blame him."

"What did you say? Are you agreeing with him?" She was on her feet, eyes blazing, hands fisted at her hips.

His eyes were equally hot. "I can't help it. If you were mine, Pru, I'd move heaven and earth to keep you safe."

She poked a finger in his chest. "You listen to me..."

Once again, the mere touch of her had him forgetting all the rules. Though he hadn't meant to, he dragged her into his arms and framed her face with his big hands, forcing her to meet his eyes. "No. You listen to me. If it meant locking you up in some private estate, away from the dangers of this world, I'd do it. And nothing you could say would change my mind." His voice lowered. "If you were mine, I'd move heaven and earth to keep you safe."

She could feel him holding himself back even as the passionate words tumbled out.

As she opened her mouth to argue, he covered her lips with his, kissing her into silence.

They were both shocked by the intensity of their feelings as they poured themselves into that single kiss. A kiss that had them trembling with need. Both of them could feel the storm building, shuddering through them, threatening to break through at any moment.

Pru pulled free, dragging air into her starving lungs. "Micah…"

"Shh." He kissed her again, softer now. Nuzzling her mouth with his until her lips softened, then opened for him.

"I'll do whatever it takes to keep you safe, Pru." He whispered the words against her mouth, then inside her mouth. "No matter the price."

His words, spoken almost reverently, set off fireworks inside her. There was such restrained passion in his tone. And beneath the steel, so much tenderness. In that moment she felt her heart fill to overflowing with love for this man. She had no doubt that he would die for her if necessary. That knowledge made her heart swell with love.

Though she knew he wanted to do more, he gathered her into his arms and pressed his mouth to a tangle of hair at her temple. "Now, if you have any feeling for me at all, Pru, you'll turn around and walk up those stairs without looking back."

"But, Micah…"

"Please."

She could see what that word cost him. Whatever protest she might have been ready to make was gone in an instant. She lifted herself on tiptoe to brush a kiss over his mouth. Then she turned and walked away.

Micah waited until he was alone. Then he turned and stared out the window at the backyard, waiting for his nerves to settle.

This was one time when shooting hoops wouldn't do a thing to calm his aggression.

There was only one cure for it. And he was honor bound to keep his distance from Pru. He was, after all, nothing more than a hired gun, paid to see to the safety of the princess in the ivory tower.

He'd try his best not to forget that in the days to come.

Chapter 14

While Prudence showered and dressed, she could hear the noise level in the house growing in volume as the others awoke and started their morning routines. To someone who had grown up in a house so quiet the scuff of a housekeeper's slippers could be heard in the hallway, this was an entirely new experience. She thought of her own apartment, where she often turned on the television just for the sound of another human voice.

By the time she started downstairs, the noise level in the kitchen was almost at a fever pitch.

She stepped inside to find Kieran at the stove calmly arranging bacon on a paper towel. Kate, dressed in a suit and simple pumps, was insisting that she didn't have time to eat. But when Kieran persisted, she reluctantly accepted a plate of scrambled eggs from his hand and headed toward the trestle table across the room.

At the table, Cam was rummaging through an attaché case, tossing papers aside in a frantic search for a particular document. When he found it, he let out a cheer and hurried out of the room to fax it to a client. When he returned, he was beaming. It occurred to Prudence that he looked far different this morning in a dark suit and conservative tie than the sweaty jock she'd met the evening before. Overnight he'd become the very model of a successful Washington lawyer.

"Here." Kieran thrust a plate of bacon and eggs into Cam's hand. "Eat."

"No time."

Cam was about to snatch up the briefcase when Kieran said, "Make time. I cooked it. You'll eat it."

Cam rolled his eyes before taking the plate to the table.

"Now you, lass." Kieran began filling a plate before Prudence could refuse.

She glanced over at Micah, who, through it all, kept a cell phone to his ear while writing furiously on a notepad. He glanced at her, winked, then returned his attention to the task at hand.

Prudence accepted the plate and trailed Cam to the table, waiting for her heart to settle. Each time Micah looked at her like that, her nerves seemed to go into a tailspin. As she took a seat, Kieran and Micah walked up to join the others.

"Do you eat like this every day?" She sat on the bench and felt a quick rush of heat as Micah moved in beside her, their thighs brushing.

"Whenever I can have my way with them." Kieran reached for the salt and pepper. "I know for a fact they never take the time to eat the rest of the day. I was raised to believe that our brains must be fed."

She glanced around the table. "If that's the case, the Lassiter brains have been well nourished. As well as their bodies."

"And not an overweight one in the bunch," Kieran said with pride. He stared pointedly at the way she was moving the food around her plate, without eating much of it. "I hope you're not one of those modern young women who believe in starving yourself to look like a model."

"Actually, I enjoy eating. But not this early in the morning." She turned to Kate. "I'd like to thank you for your hospitality. Bren's room was really comfortable."

"I'm glad you enjoyed it, Prudence. I hope this won't be the last time we see you."

Micah helped himself to toast. "Pru's leaving for Seattle right after breakfast."

She paused with her fork halfway to her mouth. "I'm what?"

He bit into his eggs. "I just got off the phone with your father. He's determined that you return to Seattle. We'll be leaving for the airport right after we eat."

"We?" Her tone grew frigid. "Are you thinking of accompanying me?"

"No. I'll be in Georgetown, working with your father's security team and the FBI until we find this guy."

"This guy." She set down her fork and turned her head to study him. "Do you realize you haven't told me a single thing about this 'guy' you're after. Not who he is, or what his threat was. Nothing, except that you've been hired to see that I'm kept safe."

Micah glanced around the table and saw that his family had gone silent, watching and listening with avid interest. "I think you should hear this from your father, Pru."

"My father isn't here. You are." She folded her arms over her chest. "I'm listening."

"Okay." He shoved aside his plate. "Your father has been getting Internet threats from a person who believes that the software package made by your father's company has the capability to spy on him. This guy is convinced that his computer is sending back personal information about him to your father's company.''

''That's crazy.''

''Yeah.'' Micah's eyes narrowed. ''That's what makes him so dangerous. He really believes that stuff. What's worse is that he appears to be smart enough to break through your father's personal passwords, and now smart enough to find you. That makes him doubly dangerous. We know we have to work quickly to get this guy. Until we do, you'll be safe at your father's estate in Seattle.''

She leaned back, shaking her head. ''I'm not going to Seattle, Micah.''

He huffed out a tired breath. ''I've been on the phone for the past hour, while your father rearranged his entire schedule in order to bring you back to Seattle. He wants you home today.''

''Washington is my home now. I'm not leaving.''

''Fine.'' He handed her his cell phone. ''Then you can be the one to tell your father.''

''I will.''

As she started to dial he put a hand on her arm. ''Before you call him, I suggest you decide where you're going to stay. You can't go back to your apartment now that the security has been breached.''

She paused, considering.

''If you'd like to stay here, lass, you're more than welcome.'' Kieran looked across the table at his daughter-in-law, who nodded her agreement.

''You mean it?'' Prudence, too, glanced at Kate for confirmation.

''You're welcome to stay as long as you please.'' Kate glanced at her watch. ''Now I really have to leave.'' She grabbed up a briefcase bulging with paperwork and brushed a kiss over Kieran's cheek, before kissing her two sons and patting Pru's shoulder. ''I'll be late tonight.''

''I'll keep your supper warm.'' The old man handed her a bag.

''What's this?''

He grinned. ''Last night when you were telling us about that pretty young mother and her little ones who'd come to you for help, you mentioned that they gobbled up my egg-salad sandwich like it was gold. I made some more. See that you put them in that little box you call a refrigerator as soon as you get to your office.''

''You're a sweetheart.'' Kate kissed him again before dashing out to her car.

''She's not the only one running late.'' Cam

lifted his attaché case and turned toward the door, calling over his shoulder, ''I guess I'll see you tonight, Prudence.''

''I hope so.'' She watched him walk away before returning her attention to the phone. ''I'll just give my father the news that I won't be flying to Seattle.''

Micah walked to the counter and returned with the coffeepot. He didn't want to miss a single moment of the fireworks that were about to begin.

As Micah drove toward Georgetown, he was grinning. He'd been right about the fireworks between Pru and her father. To her credit, Pru had managed to keep her cool for almost a full minute. Her voice had been calm enough when she'd told her father that she wasn't flying back to Seattle, no matter what he had to say. It had risen only slightly when he'd reminded her how disappointed he was in her. But when Allen Street had threatened to have Micah carry her aboard the plane and accompany her to her childhood home, she'd cut him off in midsentence by hanging up the phone.

Several attempted phone calls later, Allen Street had admitted defeat. He'd agreed that she could remain in the Washington area as long as she stayed away from her apartment and her work at the Children's Village until the danger had passed.

Though she was reluctant to give up the work that meant so much to her, Prudence had agreed, for the sake of this one small victory.

Before leaving home, Micah had extracted a promise from Pru that she wouldn't leave the house. For good measure he'd asked his grandfather to stay close to home as well, since there was no telling how long this assignment might drag on.

He drove up to the nondescript building in Bethesda and flashed his identification before being admitted inside, where the FBI agents were waiting to brief him, along with Allen Street's security team, on the progress they'd made. After greeting Will Harding, Micah was introduced to the rest of the team before settling down to the serious business that had brought them together.

"Micah said you moved in here right after your son died." Prudence stashed her plate in the dishwasher.

"That's right." Kieran Lassiter looked up from the bag of apples he'd begun to wash at the sink. "I needed Kate and the kids as much as they needed me. We were all in a state of shock."

"Though I lost my mother, it was to illness, not something as shocking as a shoot-out. I can't even imagine losing my father like that. I read the newspaper account in Bren's album."

"An entire city grieved with us." Kieran pulled a stool up to the sink and began peeling the apples. "For the longest time afterward, I couldn't bring myself to read the accounts of Riordan's death. I guess it was a year or more before I finally looked through them. Kate had meticulously cut out everything she could find, so her children would have the facts when they got older." He shook his head and paused in his work. "Kate's the strongest woman I've ever met. My son made a wise choice. While the rest of us fell apart, she just carried on, doing what she had to, raising her four children, going back to school for her law degree."

Prudence rummaged in a drawer until she found another paring knife. Then she pulled up a stool and began working alongside Kieran, peeling apples. "I'm sure having you here with the kids made it easier for her."

"Maybe." He gave a snort of laughter. "But it took some adjusting for all of us. I was a lot tougher than Riordan, and the kids resented that. I'd been alone in the five years since my wife had died, and I wasn't used to having kids underfoot all day. The minute they tested my patience, I'd send them out the door to work off all that energy on hoops. Pretty soon, it became such a routine, all I had to do was give them my famous I've-had-all-I-can-take-look and they'd be out the door."

He and Prudence shared an easy laugh. She felt completely at ease with this silver-haired, courtly gentleman with the lilting voice and devilish blue eyes. It was easy to see where the Lassiters inherited their rugged good looks.

He nodded toward the apples left in the sink. "If you can finish peeling these, I'll get started on the piecrust."

"Go ahead. I can handle this."

He dusted a board with flour before taking a ball of dough from the refrigerator. "In the beginning I never expected to stay on here. I just wanted to step in and fill a void. But the longer I stayed, the more I realized this was where I wanted, and needed, to be. Of course, I wasn't so sure it was the same for Kate. After all, she was young and beautiful, and I figured if I stayed on too long I might get in the way of her personal life."

"Did she ever date?"

Kieran shook his head. "Maybe she was just too overwhelmed with law school and four kids and a busybody father-in-law, but I like to think she was just so much in love with my son, no other man appealed to her. Whatever the reason, she's never brought a man home to meet her family. And knowing the hours she works, I doubt there'd be any time left over for a love life."

"She's still beautiful."

"That she is." Kieran expertly rolled the dough and lifted it into the pie plate, then began adding the apple slices, along with sugar and cinnamon, before fitting on the top crust. "And our Bren looks just like her." He trimmed the crust, crimped the edges and set it in the oven to bake.

"Is Bren's name really Mary Brendan?"

Kieran chuckled. "After Micah and Donovan, my son had already picked out the name for his third. Brendan, after my father. When she was born, he couldn't seem to wrap his mind around a girl's name. So he just added Mary to it, and there you are."

Prudence was laughing as she cleaned out the sink and added the bowl and paring knives to the dishwasher. "Bren told me last night that she grew up feeling like one of the boys."

"That she did." Kieran washed his hands and reached for some paper toweling. "She's tough, our Bren. With a fine, quick mind. She's not one to sit back and let her brothers get the best of her."

"Why did she move out?"

He shrugged and began wiping down the counter with the paper towel. "It's time she left the nest and made a life for herself. Time for all our birds to fly. They come back often enough that Kate and I aren't feeling deserted yet. We're both a bit flattered by the fact that they enjoy being around us. But we know better than to try to hold on to them."

"How did you figure it out?"

He paused in his work. "Figure what out?"

"When it was time to let go?"

"When they started to push away." He glanced down at the wad of paper in his hand. "If we feel ourselves being smothered, it's the most natural thing in the world to push away until we can breathe." He looked over and met her eyes. "Sometimes the hardest lesson in life for parents to learn is that the tighter they hold on to their child, the more the child will push away."

Seeing the pain in her eyes, he picked up the kettle. "I don't know about you, but I'm ready for some tea before I tackle the laundry."

It was dusk when Micah turned into the driveway of his mother's house and climbed wearily from the car. Though he'd been in contact with Pru by phone, he hadn't been home in three days. Three very long, very unproductive days.

She'd been allowed to return to her apartment accompanied by an FBI agent only long enough to pack a few of her belongings. Then she'd been driven back to the Lassiter home, after being transferred to several vehicles and drivers. They were taking no chances that she might be followed.

Micah trudged up the steps of the porch. Inside he could hear the sound of feminine voices upstairs, lilting with laughter. Apparently Pru and his sister, Bren, were sharing a joke. It was good to know those two had bonded. It couldn't have been easy for someone like Pru to endure a household as busy as this. Yet whenever he'd spoken with her on the phone, he'd heard not a word of complaint.

He made his way to the kitchen, where he found his mother and grandfather sipping tea at the trestle table. They looked up when he walked in.

"Micah." Kate's smile deepened. "Kieran and I were just talking about you. Have you had dinner yet?"

"I'm not hungry."

The door opened and Prudence and Bren rushed in like two whirlwinds, followed almost immediately by Cam.

"Micah." Bren started toward him, smiling with pleasure. "Look what Pru loaned me."

He barely acknowledged his sister when he caught sight of Pru's heart-stopping smile. If only he had one of his own to share. But he was fresh out of good cheer at the moment.

"What's this?" Kate touched a hand to her daughter's sleeve.

"Cashmere. Pru said she'd be hurt if I didn't

wear her cashmere sweater. She said if she can sleep in my room, I can wear her clothes.''

Pru was still standing in the doorway, staring at Micah, without saying a word.

Cam lifted a carton of milk from the refrigerator and chugged it down. Between gulps he said, ''You ought to see Pru shoot hoops.''

Micah blinked, pulling himself back from his bleak thoughts. ''You've got her playing basketball?''

''Well, I'm not sure you could call what she does playing.'' Cam winked at his brother. ''Since Bren taught her the rules, it's a little like mortal combat. For a shy one, Pru has certainly become a fierce competitor. Not to mention that she's become almost as noisy as Bren.''

While he was talking, he realized that neither Pru nor Micah had moved. They were staring at each other as though they'd been apart for a year instead of mere days.

Seeing everyone watching her, Pru clasped her hands together and prayed her voice wouldn't tremble. ''You haven't come with good news, have you, Micah?''

He shook his head. ''It seemed good for a while. The FBI was able to come up with a detailed profile of our stalker. His name is Calvin Hoxley. A loner with no friends, and few who even know him. Considered something of a computer genius at Cal Tech. But he dropped out after just two years. Worked at a computer lab in San Francisco, but was fired when he was found to be sending threatening e-mails to the staff. A definite pattern here. He would become fixated on someone, imagine a dozen different ways he'd been insulted, then dream up ways to get even.''

"That's good news, isn't it?" Pru took a step forward. "If they know so much about him, they ought to have him in custody soon."

"I don't know about soon. The bad news is, he seems to have gone underground. By the time they got to his last known address, he'd checked out, leaving most of his belongings behind. There's no telling when he'll surface."

Pru studied Micah's grim face. "Are you saying this could take weeks? Even…months?"

He nodded. "We don't know at this point whether he's dropped out of sight because he thinks we're onto him, or whether he's just waiting to see when you return to your apartment."

"You think he's watching?"

"That's what the FBI thinks. Hoxley dropped out of sight right after that incident in your apartment. They think he's somewhere nearby, just waiting to catch a glimpse of you."

Pru crossed her arms over her chest, tapping a

foot nervously. "So he may be thinking that I've just gone away for a few days?"

"I suppose. That's what everyone at the Children's Village was told to say if anyone phoned for you."

Micah saw the way her eyes narrowed in thought.

"Then maybe it's time for me to return."

He was on his feet, eyes blazing. "Are you crazy?"

"Not crazy." Her head came up. "Angry. This man is robbing me of my hard-earned freedom. I want it back."

"And you'll get it back as soon as we catch him."

"Which could take weeks or months. I can't put my life on hold forever." She lowered her voice. "I could be the bait to catch this man."

He was already shaking his head. "Your father would never permit it."

"He would if you assured him that I wouldn't get hurt."

"I can't make that kind of assurance, Pru. Too many things can go wrong."

She caught his hands in hers. "I'll have you and my father's security team and the FBI watching over me. I'll do whatever you tell me." When he started to pull away, she stopped him, her voice pleading. "Micah, you know I don't consider myself very brave. But I'm desperate to have my life back. Let me at least meet with your people and present my idea to them. If they agree, I'll talk to my father." She took in a deep breath. "Please."

Over her head he saw his mother and grandfather exchange a look before getting up from the table to gather around her for support. Bren drew an arm around Pru's shoulders, while Cam patted her hand in an expression of sympathy.

The whole family, it seemed, had decided to take up her cause.

Seeing them, Micah gave out a long, slow sigh of defeat. "Why do I get the feeling I'm outnumbered here?"

"Because you know she's right," Kieran said gruffly.

"Maybe. But that doesn't make the decision any easier."

"Then try this," Kate said gently. "At least let Prudence talk to the others. What she's saying makes sense. She can't put her life on hold indefinitely."

"At least she still has a life. This isn't some television drama. In real life, things can go wrong. And when they do, the director isn't around to call for another take."

"I'll do whatever I'm told, Micah. You know

I'm not brave enough, or foolish enough, to tempt fate.'' Pru's eyes were wide and pleading. ''I just want to have this thing over and done with.''

Micah went very still, mulling over the idea, and hoping desperately to find flaws in it. Finally he reached for the cell phone in his pocket. ''I'll arrange a meeting.''

At Pru's exclamation he added, ''A meeting. That's all I'm promising. You're going to have to do some fast talking to sell this to the FBI.''

Chapter 15

As Pru showered and dressed, she was aware that her hands were shaking, making it difficult to button her silk blouse. She hated this fear that never seemed to leave. But at least, she consoled herself, she was finally doing something, instead of simply hiding away. She hated being a victim. Hated the feeling of powerlessness that had gripped her when she'd learned that she was being stalked. Now, no matter how afraid she was, at least she was doing something.

But was it the right thing?

She knew her father disapproved. Even after a dozen conversations with the head of the FBI team handling the case, Allen Street wasn't convinced that his daughter should be allowed to involve herself. She'd been apprised of the danger. Had been given a list of things that could go wrong. But after all that, the FBI team had admitted that she was probably the only bait that would bring this madman out of hiding.

This was her first day back on the job, and the fear was like a hard knot in the pit of her stomach. Even though she knew that she would never be alone, she felt naked and vulnerable. During the day a female operative would be assigned to her at work, playing the part of a trainee. She would accompany Pru wherever she went, even to the ladies' room. Micah intended to follow her to and from work, but always from a respectable distance, in case she was being observed by the stalker. A camera and listening device had been installed in the great room and kitchen of her apartment, with a monitor in Micah's, so that he could see and hear her. He had wanted more, but Pru had drawn the line at having a camera in her bedroom. To compensate, Micah had won another victory. Agents acting as a cleaning crew would sweep her apartment each day for bugs before she was allowed to return to it.

She knew the security people would do everything in their power to keep her safe. And though it gave her a measure of comfort, she also knew that she was completely out of her element. Her once restrictive life had become an open book. It was, she realized, going to take some getting used to.

When she picked up her purse and stepped out of her apartment, Micah's door opened and he gave her one of those heart-stopping winks. "Good morning, Ms. Street. Lovely day, isn't it?"

She managed a smile. "Yes it is. It almost makes me wish I didn't have to go to work today."

"Want to play hooky?" He touched a hand to her shoulder. Just a touch as he opened the door leading to the garage.

"Don't tempt me." She tossed her purse into her car before sliding behind the wheel.

In a voice only she could hear, he whispered, "There's still time to change your mind, Pru."

She gave a quick shake of her head. She'd fought too hard for this. There was no turning back.

As she drove away, she took comfort in the sight of Micah's car trailing behind. She glanced around at the crowds of people on street corners, dashing to their jobs. So many people. Any one of them could be the stalker. She drew in a deep breath and forced herself to think of something else. There was no point in adding to her fear.

At least, she thought as she fiddled with the buttons on the car stereo, she had reclaimed her life. She may be living with fear, but at least she was back in her apartment again, and returning to the work she loved.

She pulled into the parking lot of the Children's Village and tossed the strap of her purse over her arm as she strode purposefully to her office. This was, she reminded herself, the first day of her newly reclaimed life. She intended to make the most of it.

The day, which had begun with overcast skies, was now growing darker by the minute. As Pru drove her car through late-afternoon traffic, the streetlights had already come on. She could feel the static electricity in the oppressive air. It added to her sense of anxiety. The long hours spent at work, pretending that nothing was wrong, had been more draining than she'd anticipated. Every time a stranger walked past her door, she'd experienced a sudden rush of fear, followed by a gradual weakness in her limbs.

Coward. The word taunted her. It seemed all the more humiliating now that she'd become familiar with Micah's family. Despite the wrenching loss of their son, husband and father at the hands of a gunman, each of them had risen above their pain to take charge of their lives. All she'd had were a few veiled Internet threats, and she was shaken to her very core.

In the rearview mirror she caught sight of Micah's car trailing behind her. Here she was, surrounded by brave people willing to risk their own lives for her, and she was still afraid.

Annoyed at herself, she turned into the garage and switched off the ignition. Micah's car pulled smoothly beside hers. As they walked into the building, they were met by two agents who avoided eye contact as they passed by.

In a barely audible voice one agent whispered to Micah, "The apartment's clean."

Micah nodded and followed Pru down the hallway. At the door to her apartment he waited while she turned the key in the lock and opened the door, disarming the security alarm.

When she turned to him, he could see the flicker of fear in her eyes. He wanted to hold her, just for a moment. As much for himself as for her. But there was no time. Until this thing was over, they each had a part to play.

This thing.

He hated it. Hated what it was doing to Pru.

"Sweet dreams." He permitted himself the luxury of laying a hand over hers before turning to his own door.

As soon as he was inside, he switched on the monitor and watched as Pru dropped her purse and keys on the hall table before walking toward the kitchen.

By the time Pru had made herself a salad, the sky had turned as dark as night. Thunder rumbled in the distance and rain began pelting the windows. She turned up the volume of the stereo to drown out the storm and made herself a cup of tea. But nothing would help to settle her nerves.

She could feel all the old fears sneaking up on her, weakening her defenses.

She wrapped her arms around herself, fighting for calm. She was a grown woman. A woman trying desperately to take charge of her life. But right now, at this moment, she felt like that frightened little girl again, huddled in her mother's closet, yearning desperately for the comfort of a mother's arms.

Annoyed, she set aside her tea and made her way to the bedroom. This kind of night called for comfort clothes. A robe and slippers, and maybe a good book in bed.

At that moment, thunder crashed overhead, followed by a blinding flash of lightning. At the same instant she thought she heard a door open and close, but it was impossible to tell over the sound of the storm. Without warning, her apartment was plunged into darkness. And as she paused in the doorway leading to her bedroom, a chill raced along her spine as a hand closed over her mouth, cutting off her scream.

Micah was drinking coffee and pacing as he watched the monitor. Pru was doing her best to hide her nerves, but he could see her restlessness growing as the storm began building. Remembering her fear of storms, it took every bit of his self-control to remain in his apartment, when all he really wanted was to be with her.

He'd argued this point with the FBI, but they remained adamant that the whole point of this venture was to bring the stalker out of hiding. That would only happen if he knew Pru to be alone, and thus vulnerable to his attack.

And so Micah waited and watched and paced.

When the storm knocked out the power, sending the apartment complex into complete darkness, he let out a string of oaths as he headed for the door. Right now he didn't give a damn about the rules. He wasn't going to leave Pru alone with her demons.

Pru couldn't catch her breath. The hand covering her mouth was suffocating her. She was pinned firmly against a man's body. She could smell him. Smell the almost overpowering odor of sweat, and the thick, cloying fragrance of cheap cologne that he'd used to cover it.

Something cold was pressed to her temple and she shuddered as she realized it was a gun.

"You make one sound and it'll be your last." His whispered words reminded her of the hiss of a snake. "You understand?"

She gave a nod.

Just then there was a sharp rap on the door of her apartment, and Micah's muffled voice called, "Pru? You all right?"

Her heart leaped to her throat.

"Answer him." The man kept his hand over her mouth as he added, "And it had better be the right answer, or it'll be your last." Very slowly he removed his hand from her mouth, all the while pressing the cold steel of his gun to her temple.

"I'm..." She couldn't speak over the hard knot of fear that was choking her. She swallowed and tried again. "I'm fine, Micah."

"Open the door. I need to see for myself."

The attacker swore under his breath. "Tell him you're not dressed."

"I'm...not decent, Micah."

"All the better." There was a rumble of familiar

laughter from the hallway. "Come on, Pru. Open up. It's so dark I won't know the difference."

The attacker's hands were rough and bruising as he dragged her closer toward the door. "Get rid of him. Now. Or I'll blow him away." He took aim at the door, and Pru realized that Micah wouldn't stand a chance against an unexpected bullet.

"Micah." Pru couldn't stop her voice from trembling. It was impossible to mask her fear. "I'm fine. Really."

"I know how you feel about storms, Pru. Let me in."

"No, Micah. Please." She closed her eyes, more terrified by the threat of the gunman than she'd ever been by anyone or anything in her life. "I insist that you go away. Do you hear me?"

"Okay. If you say so." Micah's voice faded away, and a door could be heard opening and closing across the hall.

Pru's heart nearly stopped beating. The thought of facing this madman alone had her gripped by paralysis. But it was far better knowing that at least she'd managed to save Micah's life.

In the silence that followed, the stranger pressed his mouth to her temple to whisper, "That was real good."

She felt her skin crawl from the touch of him, the smell of him.

"I've been waiting for you." His voice whispered across her nerves. "I haven't eaten or slept, or even taken time to change my clothes since I was here last. But I had to see where Allen Street's daughter lived. I knew if I waited long enough you'd be back. And now here we are. Just the two of us. Now we're going to have us some fun."

He turned and began roughly dragging Pru through the darkness toward her bedroom.

Suddenly from behind them came a loud crash as the door was forced open and Micah came hurtling through the doorway.

Lightning flashed, illuminating a gun in his hand. At the same instant, he caught sight of Pru in the arms of her attacker.

As the lightning streaked away, the room was once more plunged into darkness.

The stranger's voice was low and menacing. "Drop the gun or I blow her away."

"Micah—" Her cry was cut off abruptly as she felt the cold steel of a pistol jammed painfully against her temple.

"Are you all right, Pru?" Micah cursed the darkness. He was a crack marksman. If there were any light at all, he could take out the gunman without endangering the woman in his arms. But with only the occasional burst of lightning, he knew he had no chance.

"I'm…all right, Micah." She sucked in a breath as a hand closed over her mouth.

"You heard me, hero. Drop the gun or the woman buys it right here."

Without a word, Micah tossed aside his weapon. As soon as his pistol clattered to the floor, he heard a string of oaths and an explosion of gunfire from across the room. In the next instant he felt the pain, sharp and swift, as the bullet struck him with such force he was driven backward against the wall. For a moment he saw stars and had to struggle to remain standing. If not for the wall, he would have fallen. But he knew it was only a matter of time before his legs would refuse to hold him.

In some distant part of his mind he heard Pru's scream. For Micah, that was the worst part of this. Not the pain, though it seemed to be a replay of the agony he'd suffered in the past. It was the knowledge that he was helpless to save the woman he loved from this madman.

The woman he loved.

It shook him to his very soul to know that he might never have the chance to tell her just how much she meant to him. His damnable code of honor had kept him from speaking the truth when he'd had the opportunity.

As blood streamed from his chest, his legs weakened, and he slid to the floor.

"Micah."

From somewhere nearby he heard Pru's voice. A voice on the edge of hysteria. The pain grew, and he struggled just to remain conscious. Conscious and alive. For he knew that as long as he had a breath left in his body, there was still a chance to divert the stalker's attention long enough to get Pru to safety.

That was all that mattered now. His own life meant nothing to him. He would gladly die, as long as it meant that Pru could live.

As he faded in and out of consciousness, he heard Hoxley's voice, high-pitched with elation. "Now, Allen Street is going to learn an important lesson. I warned him, but he wouldn't listen. This time, when I'm through with his sweet little daughter, he'll wish he'd paid more attention to Calvin Hoxley."

"You've killed him." Pru shrugged off the hand that covered her mouth and began weeping.

Though it was too dark to make out more than a vague shadow, Pru could see that Micah had slumped to the floor. She'd seen, too, in that one blinding flash of lightning, blood pouring from his chest.

So much blood. A torrent of it.

This was all like some horrible nightmare.

Worse, by far, than any of her childhood fears. Suddenly her own life paled into insignificance. It no longer mattered if she lived or died. Micah was dead. This courageous, noble man, who'd already put his life on the line before, was now dead because of her.

She turned to her stalker. In the occasional flash of lightning, she could see his eyes, bright with madness. Could see long dark hair that fell to his shoulders, and a bushy beard that hid the lower half of his face.

She lifted her chin. Her voice trembled, though she no longer cared if he could sense her fear. "Go ahead, then. Kill me, too."

"Oh, I intend to. But not until after—" His words were cut off as twin beams of light pierced the darkness.

"Here you are, Prudence, dear." Octavia and Odelia Vandevere stepped into Pru's apartment. Each of them was carrying a flashlight.

"That thunder sounded as loud as a cannon. Did you know your door was wide open?" Octavia flashed the light in Pru's face, then turned it on the man standing beside her. "I don't believe we've met your friend, dear."

"Oh, look, Sister." Odelia's wispy little voice lifted in surprise when she scanned the room and her light found Micah, sitting on the floor, propped up against the wall. "It's that handsome Micah Lassiter. Whatever are you doing over there, young man?"

"Is that…" Following her sister's lead, Octavia beamed her light on Micah and took a step closer. "Is that blood?"

"I'm afraid so." He was grateful when, in order to make her way to him, she was forced to lower her flashlight from his eyes and trail it across the floor.

"Oh, Micah." Across the room Pru let out a cry. "You're alive."

"Now, why wouldn't he be alive, dear?" Odelia turned her light on Pru, causing her momentary blindness.

Pru lifted a hand to her eyes to shield them. As she did so, she realized that the man beside her must also be blinded by the sudden light. She took that moment to shove him roughly aside. He was so startled, the gun dropped from his hand. Hearing it clatter at her feet, Pru fell to the floor, feeling wildly around in hopes of locating it before he did.

Her fingertips brushed something cold. Before she could pick up the gun, Calvin's hand was there, snatching it away.

"Prudence, dear." Octavia's voice lifted in alarm as she flashed the beam of light over Calvin Hoxley. "Are you and your friends playing some sort of parlor game? I believe you should tell us just what this is all about.''

''It's about an eye for an eye.'' Calvin Hoxley shoved Pru aside, and lifted the hand holding the pistol. ''Allen Street's daughter is about to atone for his sins. As for you two old biddies and our hero over there—'' he gave a shrill laugh ''—let's just say your timing was really off. This isn't going to be your lucky day. But frankly I don't care how many I take out, as long as Allen Street's daughter is the one who suffers the most.''

As he took aim at the two old women, Pru stepped in front of them. ''They have nothing to do with this. I won't let you shoot them.''

His eyes narrowed in absolute disbelief. ''You won't let me? You won't let me?'' Marching forward, he shoved her roughly out of the way. ''That's another thing you'll pay for, as soon as all this baggage is out of my way.''

''No!'' Enraged, Pru ran at him, shoving him aside just as he fired. The bullet went wild, landing in the ceiling.

He brought his arm in a wide arc, catching her on the side of the head with the gun, sending her sprawling. Seeing it, Octavia and Odelia were horrified. Without a thought to their own safety, the two old women attacked him with the only weapons they had, hitting him about the head and shoulders with their flashlights.

"Why, you old…" He slashed out, sending Octavia reeling backward. As she fell, the flashlight slipped from her hands and went dark.

At once, her sister let out a cry and dropped to her knees beside her, letting her own flashlight fall to the floor.

The room was once again plunged into total darkness.

Hoxley felt around the floor until he located one of the flashlights. When he flicked it on and pointed it at the spot where Micah had been, he found it empty.

"Looking for me?" Though Micah's right arm was useless from the bullet to his shoulder, he managed to catch the stranger with a blow to the throat that had him gasping for breath. The shock of it caused the gun and flashlight to fall from Hoxley's hands before clattering to the floor.

"Now you're a dead man." Calvin wheezed out a breath and caught Micah with a fist to the midsection that had him doubling over. He followed that with a series of blows to the back of the head that sent Micah slumping to the floor.

Micah knew he'd lost too much blood to let the fight drag on. A few minutes more and he'd be as helpless as a baby. Calling on all the strength he had left, he got to his knees.

"You want more?" As Calvin brought his booted foot up, Micah caught it, sending him sprawling.

Before he could recover, Micah was on him, his hands closing around Hoxley's throat until he went limp.

Micah rolled aside, struggling for breath. The effort had cost him dearly. Blood flowed like a river from his wound.

As he took in a deep breath, he heard Hoxley's voice, high-pitched, agitated. "You lose, hero."

Micah heard the click of the trigger as Calvin's finger closed around the gun.

Before he could squeeze off a shot, he slumped down to the floor. Pru stood over him holding the remains of a crystal vase, which she'd broken over his head.

She tossed aside the shards and picked up the gun in her trembling fingers. "You so much as move, and I'll fire this." She took a deep breath. "And believe me, I don't know the first thing about guns. So, if it's true what they say about beginner's luck, I wouldn't count on walking away if I were you."

At that moment a dozen men burst into the apartment, guns drawn.

The head of the FBI team was shouting orders to the others. Seeing them, Pru was rocked by waves of relief as she handed over the gun before dropping to her knees beside Micah.

"What took you so long?" he demanded of Will Harding.

"Sorry. We've been monitoring everything from our van down the street. At first we believed it was just the lack of power that had you not answering our calls. When we realized you weren't in your apartment, we figured out that our guy must have used the cover of the storm to slip past us." He shook his head at the amount of blood. "Hold on, Lassiter. We've got the medics on their way."

As he turned away, Pru touched a tentative hand to Micah's cheek. At first she was almost afraid to touch him. Afraid if she did, she would cause him even more pain. "Please promise me you won't die."

"I...promise."

"Are you sure, Micah? There's so much blood." She couldn't seem to stop touching him. His face. His hair. Without realizing it, she was cradling him in her arms. Tears streamed down her face, nearly blinding her. She wiped them away, leaving bloody smudges over her face.

"Shh." He lifted a hand to her cheek. "It's all...over now. You were so amazing. So brave."

"Brave?" Her tears were falling faster now. She couldn't seem to stop them, or the tremors that seemed to have taken over her entire body. "I was absolutely terrified. Not for me. But for you. And for the poor Vandevere sisters."

"You were worried about us? Isn't that sweet, Sister?"

Pru and Micah looked up as Octavia and Odelia stood over them.

Pru wiped at her tears. "Are you hurt, Octavia?"

"Not a bit, dear. I just bumped my head. That nice gentleman over there told us he's with the FBI. Sister and I haven't had this much excitement since the time we invited that handsome circus performer to one of our little parties. I believe that was in 1943, wasn't it, Odelia?"

Her sister smiled and nodded. "His outraged wife showed up and started shooting up Papa's collection of porcelain figurines."

Octavia giggled like a girl. "Nobody had told us that the pretty little thing in his show, who used to shoot cigarettes out of his mouth while blindfolded, was his wife. As I recall, he was quite pale by the time the police left, and he was forced to go home with her. Come to think of it, he had a right to be." She lowered her voice. "Is it true what that young man over there told me? You were being stalked by that nasty man?''

Pru nodded, wondering how these two could remain so calm through such a terrifying scene.

''Wait until Sister and I tell our friends about this.'' Octavia caught her sister's hand. ''Come, Odelia. I think we should go up to our apartment now that the power is back on. We'll want to look our best in case there are reporters and television cameras here later.'' She gave a quick glance at the cluster of men gathered around the handcuffed attacker. ''I'm glad you gave that disgusting man his comeuppance. He had absolutely no manners at all.''

As they walked away, an emergency medical team arrived, administering a sedative to Micah before lifting him onto a stretcher. Seeing the way he winced in pain, Pru was suddenly transformed into his fierce protector, holding his hand, smoothing the damp hair from his forehead, admonishing the medical team to treat him with more care.

Will Harding walked over to say, ''I just spoke with your father, Miss Street. We have orders to take you to the airport at once. His plane is on the way.''

She was already shaking her head firmly, and moving alongside the stretcher. ''You can tell my

father that I'm going with Micah to the hospital.
And I have no intention of leaving until he does.''

As the sedative began to fog his mind, Micah
found himself wondering what had happened to
that shy little recluse he'd been hired to protect.

He linked his fingers with hers and gave her one
of those heart-stopping grins. ''Have I told you I'm
crazy about you, Miss Street?''

''You are?'' That brought a smile despite her
tears.

''Uh-huh. Know why?''

''Why?'' Since his voice had dropped to a whisper, she was forced to bend down to hear.

He brushed his mouth over hers, sending her
heart on a quick hard tumble. ''Because you're the
bravest woman I've ever met.'' He struggled to
keep his focus, though it was getting more difficult
with every passing minute. ''Know something
else?''

''What?'' She could feel the tears starting again,
harder than ever now, and made no effort to brush
them away. These were the happiest tears she'd
ever shed.

He felt as if he were flying as they lifted him
into the ambulance and she climbed in right beside
him. ''You make one hell of a tough little bodyguard.''

It was, she thought, the nicest compliment anyone had ever paid her. And when he woke up,

she'd return the favor. Maybe she would even tell him exactly how she felt about him. But for now, she was content to hear the steady beat of his heart against her cheek. And to know that the man she loved more than life itself was still right here beside her, where he belonged.

Epilogue

"He's coming."

At Bren's shout, the entire Lassiter family streamed out of the house and stood waiting anxiously on the porch.

"Watch out for your sore ribs, bro." Cam laughed as he turned off the ignition. "The gang's all here and I'm betting you're about to be hugged to death."

Micah wasn't listening. His attention was snagged by the candy-apple-red sports car parked in the driveway. He walked up the steps and was immediately surrounded by his family and thoroughly hugged and kissed. When they finally stepped aside, he saw Pru standing to one side, her hands clasped nervously together.

He paused, unwilling to touch her. If he did, he might not be able to stop. He kept his tone deliberately bland. "I thought you were in Seattle."

"I was. My father needed to see for himself that I was all right."

"I'm surprised he let you leave. I figured by now he'd have you under lock and key."

"He tried. But I think he's finally coming to the realization that I have the right to my own life."

"Well," Kieran led the way inside, "it's good to have all our chicks back home, isn't it, Katie girl?"

Kate laughed and looped her arm through her daughter's. "It is indeed."

As Cam trailed the others he lifted his head. "Do I smell pot roast?"

"You do." Kieran Lassiter was grinning from ear to ear. "I thought Micah's first day home from the hospital called for something special."

Micah forced a smile as he headed toward the kitchen. Once inside he eased himself into a seat at the trestle table and watched a scene that had been playing since his childhood. Kieran was carving the roast beef. Kate was removing a pan of perfectly browned biscuits from the oven and arranging them in a linen-lined basket. Bren stood at the mixer, mashing potatoes with milk and butter until they were smooth as silk. Cam was busy opening a bottle of wine. And there, working in their midst, as though she'd been doing it all her life, was Pru, stirring gravy at the stove, before pouring it into the ancient gravy boat that had once belonged to his grandmother.

Watching her, he felt a sudden, unexpected jolt in the heart.

Cam began passing out glasses of wine. When everyone had one in hand he lifted his. "Here's to Micah and Pru. According to a couple of old women who live in Pru's building, these two fought the enemy like a couple of marines."

Pru put a hand to her mouth. "Oh, dear. The Vandevere sisters will tell everyone in Washington."

"They already have." Bren couldn't help laughing at the frown on her brother's face. "You know how Washington loves its gossip. Octavia and Odelia have become the darlings of the media. Not to mention being prized guests at every party in Georgetown. And the two of you have become their favorite topic of conversation."

Micah glanced at Pru, who looked thunderstruck. "So much for your anonymity."

Kieran cleared his throat. "You could always change your name, lass."

Instead of the expected blush, Pru merely smiled. "I've been thinking that very thing, Pop."

Her words had Micah's frown deepening. Pop? She was beginning to sound like one of the family. Not that he wouldn't love that. But it was nothing more than a foolish dream.

Who would have believed that a simple assignment would turn into something so complicated? The woman he'd been hired to guard had somehow managed to sneak past all his defenses, until she'd become the great love of his life. That ought to be simple enough. But the fact that she was the daughter of one of the richest men in the country made the entire situation impossible.

His stay in the hospital had given him plenty of time to take a cold, hard look at himself and realize that he had nothing to offer a woman like Prudence Street. It hadn't been an easy decision. But he knew, for her sake, he needed to take a step back and give her the space she needed.

Too agitated to sit still, he got to his feet and crossed to the back door. "Think I'll shoot some hoops."

While the others continued with their chores, Pru paused by the window to watch as Micah dribbled the ball, then gingerly shot it through the basket. When it dropped through the hoop, he caught it and did the same thing again and again, wincing with each shot until the back of his shirt gradually became damp with sweat. She could see the effort each toss of the ball cost him.

Without a word she slipped away from the others and walked outside.

Micah glanced at her, then away as he took the ball in for another layup. When the ball dropped through the hoop, she stepped in front of him and caught it. Though her moves weren't as smooth as his, she managed to dodge him and toss the ball. It fell cleanly through the basket. When he went to retrieve it, she danced ahead of him and took it away.

Instead of dribbling it, she held it firmly against her chest and turned to face him. "Have you worked off enough frustration?"

"No. Toss me the ball, Pru."

She clutched it to her. "If you want it, you have to come and get it."

He shook his head and hung back.

Her chin came up in that angry way he'd come to recognize. "You haven't said one kind word to me since you came home, Micah."

Nerves made his tone harsher than he'd intended. "What would you like me to say?"

"How about I love you." She studied his eyes. "Or was that a lie, spoken in a moment of madness?"

"You know it wasn't."

"I don't know anything of the kind. One day you're declaring your love, and the next you're acting like I don't even exist." She took a step closer. "You haven't even touched me."

"Don't." He held up his hands. His voice sounded weary. "Don't push your luck, Pru."

Her eyes blazed. "It's taken me a lifetime to find my courage, Micah. But now that I have, I'm not going to back down. Not when something this important is hanging in the balance." She took in a deep breath. "I know that my father's wealth can be intimidating."

"Now, there's an understatement."

"Ah. So now we get to the heart of the matter. All my life, it's always been about money. I've been forced to lead a less-than-normal life because of my father's wealth. I was even stalked and threatened because of it. Are you now telling me that the very courageous Micah Lassiter is afraid of that same wealth?"

"Afraid? Maybe *ashamed* is a better word. I've been behaving like a high-school jock trying to impress the class valedictorian with my muscles. That's about all I have to offer someone like you, Pru."

"Someone like me?" She gripped the ball so tightly her knuckles were white. "Just what do you see when you look at me, Micah? A rich man's spoiled daughter?''

"Of course not." His voice lowered with feeling. "That may be what I'd expected. But what I discovered was this smart, funny, warm woman. A woman who showed amazing courage under fire."

"I told you, Micah. I wasn't brave. I was desperate."

"You were heroic. You stepped in front of the two Vandevere sisters, refusing to let that madman shoot them. If that wasn't courage, I don't know what is. And if that wasn't enough, you fought for my life, too."

"How could I not, when you were risking your life for me?"

In the heat of their argument he forgot all his good intentions and touched a hand to her arm. Just a touch, but he could feel the rush of heat all the way to his heart. "All I know is, the moment I saw you in the arms of that madman, I realized how desperately I loved you. And for the first time in my life, I was afraid. Afraid that I wouldn't be able to save you."

"You just said it again."

"Said what?"

"That you love me."

"Maybe I do. But that doesn't change anything.

Love alone isn't enough. You're still Allen Street's daughter. And I'm still just a working stiff.''

"I see. And you think that makes me too good for you. Or maybe you think you're too good for me." She took a step back, breaking contact. "Thank heaven not all the Lassiter men are as bull-headed as you. I guess I'll have to go with plan B."

"Plan B?" His eyes narrowed.

"I've already decided that I want to be part of this family. I've fallen in love with all of them. So if you won't marry me, I'll ask your grandfather. He's already admitted a special fondness for me. And I doubt he'd be intimidated by my father's money, or by anything that stood in the way of what he wanted."

As she started to turn away, he caught her by the arm and spun her back. "That isn't funny, Pru."

"I didn't intend it to be." She held herself stiffly. "If you won't have me, I'll find someone who will."

"It isn't that easy."

"Oh yes it is." She shoved the basketball into his chest and stepped back. "If you really loved me, you'd find a way to make it work, instead of looking for every obstacle you can find."

"Is that what you think? That I'm looking for a

way out?'' He tossed the ball aside and started after her. ''The problem is, I have nothing to offer you.''

He had his hands on her before he could stop himself. His fingers tingled from the contact as he ran them up her arms, across her shoulders, all the while staring down into those wide amber eyes. ''All I have is a heart filled to overflowing with love for you. What is that compared to what you deserve?''

''What is that? Oh, Micah.'' She wrapped her arms around his waist and lifted herself on tiptoe to reach his mouth. ''Your love, your heart, are all I want. All I'll ever want.''

He couldn't resist brushing his lips to a tangle of hair at her temple. ''How can you be so sure? What if you wake up one morning and regret the life you left behind?''

''You mean the silence and the loneliness?''

''I was thinking more about the private jet and unlimited expense accounts.''

''Those are just things, Micah. They can't take the place of love.''

''Are you sure?''

''More sure than I've ever been of anything in my life.''

''I love you, Pru.'' He spoke the words against

her lips. "More than life itself. You'd make me the happiest man in the world if you'd marry me."

"Oh, Micah. With that damnable honor you wear like a badge, I was afraid you'd never ask."

As they came together in a hot, hungry kiss, they could hear the sound of muffled cheering. They both looked up to see the Lassiter family peering at them through the window.

Pru's eyes widened. "They were listening."

"It's an old family weakness. Come on." He caught her hand.

"Where are we going?"

"I think it's time I showed you my house down the street. It'll be a lot more private for what I have in mind. And believe me, right now I'm craving a whole lot of privacy. Do you know how long it's been since I've held you? Loved you?"

She touched a hand to his chest. "Are you sure you're strong enough?"

"Trust me." He shot her a look that would melt glaciers. "I'm more than ready to sacrifice myself for the cause."

As they started away, he shouted over his shoulder, "Don't hold dinner. We have some very important business to take care of."

"Micah." Laughing, Pru tugged on his hand, stopping him in the driveway.

He drew her close and kissed her until they were

both breathless. Against her lips he whispered, "I have a whole lot of loving stored up for you, Miss Street. And if we can ever tear ourselves apart, we'll get down to marriage plans. Knowing the Lassiter clan, I'm assuming they'll be large and lavish. Heaven help you, you're about to become one of us."

One of us.

As she melted into him, she realized that he couldn't imagine just how sweet those words were to the sheltered only child of an overprotective father.

"I love you, Micah Lassiter. And I love your entire family."

"I'll remind you of that the first time they all swoop around the dinner table like a swarm of hungry locusts." He kept his arm firmly around her waist as they started down the sidewalk toward his house.

They were, he realized, heading toward their future.

With this amazing woman beside him, he couldn't wait for it to begin.

* * * * *

Silhouette®

INTIMATE MOMENTS™
is proud to present

Romancing the Crown

*With the help of their powerful allies,
the royal family of Montebello is determined
to find their missing heir. But the search for the
beloved prince is not without danger—or passion!*

**This exciting twelve-book series begins in January and
continues throughout the year with these fabulous titles:**

Available at your favorite retail outlet.

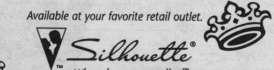

Silhouette®
Where love comes alive™

CALL THE ONES YOU LOVE OVER THE HOLIDAYS!

Save $25 off future book purchases when you buy any four Harlequin® or Silhouette® books in October, November and December 2001,

PLUS

receive a phone card good for 15 minutes of long-distance calls to anyone you want in North America!

WHAT AN INCREDIBLE DEAL!

Just fill out this form and attach 4 proofs of purchase (cash register receipts) from October, November and December 2001 books, and Harlequin Books will send you a coupon booklet worth a total savings of $25 off future purchases of Harlequin™ and Silhouette® books, AND a 15-minute phone card to call the ones you love, anywhere in North America.

Please send this form, along with your cash register receipts as proofs of purchase, to:
In the USA: Harlequin Books, P.O. Box 9057, Buffalo, NY 14269-9057
In Canada: Harlequin Books, P.O. Box 622, Fort Erie, Ontario L2A 5X3
Cash register receipts must be dated no later than December 31, 2001.
Limit of 1 coupon booklet and phone card per household.
Please allow 4-6 weeks for delivery.

**I accept your offer! Enclosed are 4 proofs of purchase.
Please send me my coupon booklet
and a 15-minute phone card:**

Name: _____

Address: _____ City: _____

State/Prov.: _____ Zip/Postal Code: _____

Account Number (if available): _____

---

097 KJB DAGL
PHQ4013

If you enjoyed what you just read,
then we've got an offer you can't resist!

Take 2 bestselling
love stories FREE!
Plus get a FREE surprise gift!

Welcome to

Silhouette®

DREAMSCAPES...

a world where passion and danger mingle together...and the temptation of dark, sensual romance awaits.

In December 2001, look for these four alluring romances:

FROM A DISTANCE by Emilie Richards

THE PERFECT KISS by Amanda Stevens

SEA GATE by Maura Seger

SOMETHING BEAUTIFUL by Marilyn Tracy

Available at your favorite retail outlet.